DEAT

She thought she had l̶̶̶̶̶̶̶̶̶̶
exhibit. But the Hunter was not so easily
smarted. Past the crowd, he saw the single door. He
went through it, to find himself in the midst of a
display of wax dummies.

He gazed at this display, searching, till, at the feet
of one of the models, he saw a telltale black sable
coat. Immediately, his camera gun was raised and
positioned. He touched the firing stud and blasted
away. It was done, he had accomplished the kill, he
had succeeded, he—

One of the other wax dummies came suddenly to
life. It was Caroline, the upper half of her body
concealed only by a strangely shaped metal bras-
siere. As she faced the startled Hunter, each breast
fired a single shot. Now on to the tenth Hunt . . .

ROBERT SHECKLEY is best known for his off-beat,
witty short stories, which he began writing in 1951. He
was a protege of Horace Gold, former editor of
Galaxy, the magazine in which many of his early
stories appeared. But by the mid-1960s, Sheckley had
already produced a significant body of work that was
widely acknowledged to be at the forefront of science
fiction. His science fiction bestseller, THE 10TH
VICTIM, and the subsequent movie launched his repu-
tation far beyond genre classification. Mr. Sheckley has
also had a major influence on his fellow writers as
fiction editor of *Omni* magazine. At present he is at
work on HUNTER/VICTIM, the third book in the
series begun with THE 10TH VICTIM and continued
with VICTIM PRIME.

◎ SIGNET SCIENCE FICTION

COME OUT OF THIS WORLD

THE 10TH VICTIM

ROBERT SHECKLEY

A SIGNET BOOK

NEW AMERICAN LIBRARY

For Alissa

NAL BOOKS ARE AVAILABLE AT QUANTITY DISCOUNTS WHEN USED
TO PROMOTE PRODUCTS OR SERVICES. FOR INFORMATION PLEASE
WRITE TO PREMIUM MARKETING DIVISION, NEW AMERICAN
LIBRARY, 1633 BROADWAY, NEW YORK, NEW YORK 10019.

SIGNET TRADEMARK REG. U.S. PAT. OFF. AND FOREIGN COUNTRIES
REGISTERED TRADEMARK—MARCA REGISTRADA
HECHO EN CHICAGO, U.S.A.

SIGNET, SIGNET CLASSIC, MENTOR, ONYX, PLUME, MERIDIAN
and NAL BOOKS are published by NAL PENGUIN INC.,
1633 Broadway, New York, New York 10019

First Signet Printing, September, 1987

1 2 3 4 5 6 7 8 9

PRINTED IN THE UNITED STATES OF AMERICA

Rules of the Hunt

The Hunt is open to anyone 18 years of age or older, regardless of race, religion, or sex.

Once you join, you're in for all ten Hunts, five as Victim, five as Hunter.

Hunters receive the name, address, and photograph of their victim.

Victims are only notified that a Hunter is after them.

All kills must be performed in person, i.e., by the Hunter or Victim himself, no proxies.

There are severe penalties for killing the wrong person.

Enrollees must continue for 10 Hunts, five as Victim, five as Hunter.

A Tens winner is awarded almost unlimited civil, financial, political, and sexual rights.

The Hunt:
1990–2150

The Hunt has gone through various stages since its beginning in the early 1990s.

It had its origin in a practice dear to the human heart: the righting of wrongs by violent means.

Back in those early days, everyone wanted to be a Hunter. No one wanted to be a Victim. The peculiar social and psychological rewards of Victim status were discovered only later, in its intermediate period, when the Hunt was set up on a new basis, with random selection and pairing of Hunters and Victims.

Due to the scarcity of volunteer Victims, the Hunt Organization selected its first victims from those groups who engaged in violence on a regular basis. These people were, for the most part, death squad participants and terrorists of all political persuasions. They were aggressors who never seemed to get aggressed upon.

Therefore the Hunt Commission thought it appropriate that they should be chosen as Victims, without, however, the latter-day formality of advance warning.

This went against the Hunt ethic. But The Organization had to produce "motivated killers" (very much against its own aesthetic) in order to find people who would proceed with killing.

The Hunters back then were what we would call "motivated" killers. In those days there was very little understanding of the purity of the Hunt, its austere ethic. It would need a later age to perceive in the Hunt

4

the ultimate art form and to refine the rules so that personal motives could play no part.

Today we can recognize a spiritual quest for what it is. It is true that some of the early Hunters thought their Hunts were motivated by the desire for revenge, "to get even," as one of them said. But we know better today. In those crude Hunts of the 1990s we recognize the dawn of the modern consciousness, the search for the ultimate purity, the conscious acceptance of man's place on the great turning wheel of life and death. The Hunt answered the call of our predator destiny—the law of nature that says that hunting animals, too, can know satori, but only through the perfect practice of their killing art.

Even in those early days, much of our present day Hunt structure was already in place. The awarding of bonus money, for example, from funds put up by rich liberals. The use of Spotters to help a Hunter or Victim locate their aggressor. The Hunt Committee tried to maintain some degree of impartiality even in those early days of "righteous killings."

What was apparent even then was the Hunt's long-range goal: to convert mankind away from its addiction to mass war by giving it instead the individual two-person death-duel as a panacea for all its woes.

Today, war is as unthinkable as the institution of the Hunt was in the 1990s.

In the Hunt's intermediate stage, during the brief hectic flourishing of Esmeralda, the new rules had just come into being, but they were still flexible. Perhaps some ambiguity was necessary: the Hunt was not universal yet, but was legal only in a single island republic, Esmeralda in the Caribbean, where it was not only the national pastime, but also provided most of the income. This came from tourists who flocked to the island from all over the world, some to Hunt, others to watch the various contests around them. All took vicarious pleasure in the death of others, and an international audience could watch the infamous Games with their shocking Big Payoff. Watch and enjoy.

Hunters in the earliest days, in the 1990s, had to contend with a population not yet completely in favor of the Hunt. Although most people found it attractive to one degree or other, the various forces of law and order disapproved and were constantly on the lookout for participants. The police back then tended to treat a Hunter much like any other common criminal.

After many centuries we have rediscovered nature's way of keeping populations in hand. Nature does it the old-fashioned way, by killing people.

So much of the literature of the 20th and 21st centuries had to do with lonely people growing older and eking out their miserable, solitary existences. That would be unthinkable nowadays. The level of the Hunt has risen to such an extent that old people don't last long: they don't have the speed or agility to scramble away from the gunfire that fills our streets as rain once did.

Children, conversely, show themselves to be extremely adroit at staying out of the line of fire.

Nobody says any longer, "When will the killing stop?"

Now we know that the killing will stop only when life itself stops.

1

She might have been any man's fatality: Caroline Meredith, a slim and lissome young lady seated pensively behind a high mahogany bar, her slim legs wrapped enraptured one around the other, her long, exquisitely carved face (reminiscent of antique jade, yet colored the faintest of ivories) directed downward into the unfathomable depths of her Martini. Statuelike, yet disturbingly alive, clad in the loveliest of silks, and with a jet black sable coat flung carelessly over her superb shoulders, she might have stood for all that was fine, good, and desirable in the strangely disparate city of New York.

Or so the tourist must have thought. He stood entranced, ten feet from the plate glass window of the bar in which the beautiful Caroline sat staring into the depths of her drink. He was a Chinese—a bird's nest salesman from Kweiping, to judge by his white sharkskin suit, shantung tie, and brocaded shoes. Slung around his neck was a large camera—a Bronica, to all but the initiated.

With elaborate carelessness the wily Oriental lifted his camera and snapped a picture of a gutter to his left and of an excavation to his right. Then he focused on Caroline.

He performed various operations with the camera's mechanism. Things whirred and buzzed, and a panel in the side flipped open.

Into this opening, with the speed of a conjurer, the inscrutable celestial deftly slipped five hollow-point bullets, and closed the aperture. Thus, technically, his camera was no longer simply a camera; but neither was it simply a gun. It was now a gun-camera, or camera-gun; or, to use the proper (though recently coined) slang term, it was a *convertible;* which is to say, one of that class of objects designed to perform two unrelated functions.

Loaded for bear, the Yellow Peril moved toward his target with light quick steps. Only slightly asthmatoid breathing might have betrayed his purpose to the casual eye.

Still the lovely Caroline kept both her pose and her poise. She lifted her drink; within there was no sibyl, but the next best thing: a tiny mirror. In it she watched with interest the actions of the killer from Kwangtung.

The moment of truth was now fast approaching. The Chinese took aim; and Caroline, with an impressive show of reflexes, hurled her drink at the window just an instant before the son of heaven got off his shot.

"Oh! Really now! I say!" the Chinese said. (Although born on the left bank of the Hungshui River, he had been educated at Harrod's.)

Caroline said not a word. One foot above her head there was a starred hole in the plate glass window. On the other side of the window was an embarrassed Chinaman. Caroline dropped to the floor before the fellow could fire again, and scooted toward the rear like a bat out of hell.

The bartender, who had been watching the action, shook his head with admiration. He was a football fan himself, but he loved a good Hunt.

"That's one for you, kid!" he called after the speeding Caroline.

Just then the bird's nest salesman burst into the bar and raced to the rear in pursuit of the beautiful running girl.

"Welcome to America," the bartender called after him. "And happy hunting."

"Sank you, I am so preased," the Yellow Devil replied politely, while sprinting full out.

"You gotta hand it to them Chinks," the bartender remarked to a customer at the far end of the bar. "They got manners."

"Another double Martini," the man at the end of the bar replied. "But this time put the twist of lemon peel *on the side.* I mean to say, one doesn't like to have a big ugly slice of lemon floating around as though one's drink were a Planter's Punch or some such vile concoction."

"Yes sir, terribly sorry, sir," the bartender said with evident good nature. He mixed the drink with care, but all the time he was wondering about that Oriental Hunter and his American Victim. Which of them was going to get it? How would it turn out?

The man at the bar must have been reading his mind. "I'll give you three to one," he said.

"On who?"

"The chick over the Chink."

The bartender hesitated, then smiled, shook his head, and served the drink. "Make it five to one," he said. "That little lady looked to me like she knew a thing or two."

"Done," said the man, who also knew a thing or two. He squeezed a fractional drop of oil over the pellucid surface of his drink.

Long legs flashing, sable coat clutched beneath one arm, Caroline ran past the tawdry splendors of Lexington Avenue and fought her way through a crowd gathered to watch the public impalement of a litterbug on the great granite stake at 69th and Park. No one even remarked on Caroline's progress; their eyes were intent on the wretched criminal, a lout from Hoboken with a telltale Hershey paper crumpled at his feet and with chocolate smeared miserably on his hands. Stony-faced they listened to his specious excuses, his pathetic pleas; and they saw his face turn a mottled gray as two public executioners lifted him by the arms and legs and lifted him high in the air, positioned for the final plunge onto Malefactor's Stake. There was a good deal of interest just then in the newly instituted policy of open-air executions ("What have we got to be ashamed of?") and not much current interest in the predictably murderous antics of Hunters and Victims.

Caroline ran on, her blonde hair swinging free like a bright flag of uncertain import. Less than 50 feet behind her, puffing slightly and perspiring faintly, came the heathen Chinee, his camera-gun gripped in both his hairless hands. His stride did not seem particularly rapid; and yet, bit by bit, with the immemorial patience of the children of Han, he was overtaking the beautiful young girl.

He risked no shot as yet; to fire without definite aim was frowned upon, and to kill or maim a bystander, no matter how accidentally, was shameful, and would constitute an irrevocable loss of face as well as a stiff fine.

Therefore he held his fire and clutched to his chest that instrument which was capable, through the perverse ingenuity of man, of simultaneously creating a copy and destroying the original. A close observer might have noticed a premonitory digital tremor, as well as a slightly unnatural stiffening of the man's neck muscles. But this was only to be expected, since John Chinaman had a mere two Hunts under his belt, and was therefore a rank beginner in the most important social phenomenon of the age.

Caroline came to Madison Avenue and 69th Street, cast a quick glance around her, went uptown past the Craven Chicken Delicatessen (Catering for up to 50 people; prices on request) and then stopped suddenly. Panting heavily and beautifully, she saw an open door just past the Craven Chicken. Instantly she entered and raced up the steep steps to the second floor, where she found herself upon a crowded landing.

At the far end of the landing she saw a sign: Gallerie Amel: *Objets de pop-op revisité*. And she knew at once that she was in an art gallery—a place she had always planned one day to visit, though under somewhat better circumstances. . . .

Still—one kills where one can and dies where one must, as the old saying has it. Therefore, without a backward glance, Caroline pushed her way to the head of the line, ignored the outraged mutters of the incensed standees, and showed a card to the uniformed attendant who was controlling and calming the human traffic.

The attendant glanced at the card, with one of which each Victim (as well as each Hunter) is issued, allowing them Emergency Rights of Ingress or Egress while actively and legally engaged in saving their own lives or destroying another's. He nodded. Caroline took back her card and entered the gallery.

She forced herself to slow down, to pick up a catalogue, to make some attempt to control her breathing. She put on a pair of glasses, pulled her coat more tightly around her rounded shoulders and moved slowly through the conjoined rooms of the gallery.

Her glasses, lightly tinted, were the recently devised "See-Around" model, which afforded the wearer an approximation of 360-degree vision, with minor but annoying blind spots at 42 and 83 degrees, and with an area of distortion extending straight ahead from 350 to 10 degrees. But even though the glasses were annoying and capable of producing severe headaches, there was no denying their usefulness. For through them Caroline spotted her Hunter some 30 feet behind her.

Yes, it was he, her own Asiatic plague, his white suit drenched with perspiration and his shantung tie pulled slightly awry. But his lethal camera was still clutched tightly to his chest, and he moved forward with the relentless stalk of a feral beast, his eyes narrowed from slits to crannies and his smooth high forehead creased in concentration.

Caroline moved with casual haste, putting a crowd of art viewers between herself and her North Kwangtung nemesis.

But John Chinaman had seen, and now he moved straight toward the crowd behind which Caroline had taken refuge. His lips were tightly compressed, and his eyes had narrowed still further, to the point where he could see very little.

But he *could* see that his Victim was not in the crowd. She had eluded him, she had gone. . . . Ah, even so! A smile tugged at the corners of his mouth. Past the crowd there was a single door. Upon seeing it, he arrived at the solution to his problem in a sudden satorilike flash of intuition, with no need for the tedious intermediate steps of Western-style logic. She had gone *in there!* And so, grimly, but with a faint hint of future compassion, he also went *in there*.

He found himself staring at a display of wax dummies—real wax, apparently, the same substance that had been used in the Time of the Ancients. He stared at the dummies, decompressing the muscles around his eyes to afford himself better vision. The figures were all of women, very attractive (by Western standards) and scantily clad (by any standards). They seemed to be portraying various postures of a dance of some sort. "Strip-tease," the placard proclaimed, "the Spurious Metamorphosis. 1945: Age of

Innocence; 1965: Rust and Moth; 1970: Renascence of Cartilege; 1980: Informal Defiance of Formality. . . ."

He gazed upon this scene, and found it barely comprehensible to eyes trained to recognize the beauty of lacquered forests, miniature stillborn rivers, stylized clutching cranes. . . . But there was one thing he did recognize.

One of those models, the third from the left, had a long blonde bang half hiding her face; and at her feet was that telltale black sable coat.

The celestial hesitated no longer. His camera-gun was raised and positioned. He touched the firing stud and blasted away, three shots grouped in a two-inch circle around the midriff; nice work by anybody's standards.

So it was done, he had accomplished the kill, he had succeeded, he—

One of the wax dummies on the far end of the line came suddenly and disconcertingly to life. The dummy whirled; it was Caroline, half clad, the upper half of her comely body concealed only by a strangely shaped metal brassière reminiscent of the one worn by Wilma, the legendary wife of Buck Rogers.

Caroline's was a more practical garment than that archetypical brassière of yore; for as she faced the startled Hunter, each breast piece fired a single shot. And the Hunter barely had time to say, "Even so, one begins to understand," before he keeled over, as dead as yesterday's mackerel in today's fish store.

A number of onlookers had, of course, been looking on. Now one remarked to another: "I consider that a *vulgar* kill."

The spoken-to replied: "Not in the slightest. It's a *campy* kill, if you will forgive the archaism."

"Neat but gaudy," the first replied. "One could, I suppose, call it a *fin de siècle* kill. Eh?"

"Most assuredly," the second onlooker replied, "if one had a taste for baggy-pants analogy."

Crushed, the first onlooker turned away with hauteur and began examining a retrospective display of NASA products.

Caroline retrieved her black sable (which several women in the audience had recognized as dyed muskrat), blew smoke from the twin recessed barrels of her breast-piece guns, pulled her clothing into order, picked up her coat, and stepped down from the mannequin dais.

The crowd, for the most part, had ignored the entire business; these were the genuine art lovers who would not allow their esthetic contemplations to be disturbed by minor and external matters.

A policeman arrived with all deliberate speed, walked up to Caroline and asked: "Hunter or Victim?"

"Victim," Caroline said, and gave him her card.

The policeman nodded, bent down over the Chinese's body and removed his wallet. Within it he found a similar card. Upon it he marked a large X. On Caroline's card he punched a star-shaped hole beneath a row of similar holes, then handed her back her card.

"Nine hunts, eh, miss?" he said in an avuncular manner.

"That's right, Officer," Caroline said demurely.

"Well, that's real nice going and you made a real nice kill," the policeman said. "Not a messy butcher's job like some people do. Personally, I like to see a good workmanlike job, in killing or cooking or repairing shoes or anything else. Now then, what do you want to do about the prize money?"

"Oh, just have the Ministry credit it to my account," Caroline said.

"I'll notify them," the policeman said. "Nine kills! Just one more to go, huh?"

Caroline nodded. By now a small crowd had formed around her, pushing the policeman out of the way. They were all women; a female Hunter was not unknown, but was still rare enough to cause attention.

They babbled their appreciation, and Caroline accepted it graciously for several minutes. But then she found that she was very tired. No normal person ever becomes completely inured to the emotional drain of a kill.

"Thank you all very much," she said, "but now I really must go home and lie down. Mr. Policeman, would you mind terribly sending me the Hunter's necktie? I'd like it for a souvenir."

"To hear is to obey," the policeman replied promptly, and he cleared a way for her through the maddening throng, which followed her all the way to the nearest taxi.

Five minutes later a small bearded man wearing a corduroy suit and French pumps entered the room. He gazed around, bewildered, at the empty gallery; hadn't they said this show was going to be a sellout? Never mind. He began examining the exhibits.

He nodded knowingly as he passed the various paintings, statues, and exhibits. He stopped when he came to the Chinese corpse, sprawled in the middle of the floor and still bleeding slightly. He stared at it long and thoughtfully, looked for and did not find it in his catalogue, and decided it must have arrived too late to be listed. He looked closely, thought deeply, and then made up his mind.

"Merely architectonic," he stated authoritatively. "Effective, perhaps, but only barely this side of maudlin."

He passed on into the next room.

2

What is so fair as a day in June? Today we can answer that question both qualitatively and definitively. Fairer by far is a day in Rome in mid-October, when Venus is ascendant in the House of Mars, and the tourists, lemminglike, have completed their mysterious annual migration and are now (most of them) homeward bound to the dank and wretched lands that gave them birth.

Some of these seekers after sunlight and the illusion of warmth stay on, however. They give their pitiable excuses: a play, a party, a concert one should not miss, an audience with this one or that one. But the real reasons are always the same. Rome has an *ambiance*, puerile yet unmatchable. Rome hints at the possibility of becoming the main actor in the drama of one's own life. (The hint is false, of course; but the stolider northern cities do not even possess the hint.)

Baron Erich Seigfried von Richtoffen was thinking of none of this. His features portrayed little except an habitual irritation. Germany annoyed him (slackness), France disgusted him (filthiness), and Italy both annoyed and disgusted him (slackness, filthiness, egalitarianism, decadence). He came to Italy every year; despite its irreparable faults, it was one of the least revolting places he could think of. And besides, it had the annual International Horse Show in the Piazza di Sienna.

The baron was a superb horseman. (Had not his ancestors trampled peasants into the mud beneath the ironclad hooves of their destriers?) He was in the stables now, and he could hear a fanfare of trumpets as the mounted carabinieri paraded through the piazza in their resplendent uniforms.

The baron was *extremely* irritated just at the moment, for he was standing in his stocking feet and waiting for one of the grooms (you can never find those fellows when you need them) to bring back his boots. The accursed fellow had been gone for 18 minutes, 32 seconds, according to the Accutron on the baron's wrist; how long did it take to shine a pair of boots? In Germany (or rather, in the town Richtoffenstein, which the baron considered the only remaining fragment of the true Germany), boots could be shined to near perfection in an average time of 7 minutes 14 seconds. This sort of delay made a man want to weep or rage, or intimidate someone, or do something. . . .

"Enrico!" the baron shouted, in a voice that could have been heard as far afield as the Campo di Mars. "Enrico, blast your eyes, where are you!"

Someone calling, no reply. . . . In the piazza, a fancy dude of a Mexican was bowing to the judges. It was the baron's turn next. But he had no boots, damn it, he had no boots!

"Enrico, you scum, advance yourself to this place on the instant or there will be blood shed this night!" the baron shouted. It was a long sentence to shout, and he was quite winded at the end of it. He listened for a reply.

And where was the elusive Enrico? Under the grandstand, putting the final gloss on a pair of riding boots so beautiful that they could not help but put any rider to shame. Enrico was a wizened old man, originally from Emilia, brought to Rome by popular demand. It was generally acknowledged that no one knew as much about the art of polishing (not even those adepts who followed the Zen Approach to the Art of Gloss) as Enrico.

Enrico worked away, concentrating now on

the gleaming spurs. His forehead was wrinkled with worry as he gently coated the silvery steel with a lustrous steely silver substance.

He was not alone. Beside him, looking on with a definite degree of interest, was a man who might have been taken for Enrico's identical twin. The two men were dressed alike down to the last shoddy detail. The only thing that set them apart was the fact that the second Enrico was bound and gagged.

Outside, the crowd roared its approval of the Mexican's performance. Above its roar could be heard the baron's parade-ground bellow:

"Enrico!"

Now, hastily, Enrico #1 rose to his feet, gave the boots a last inspection, patted Enrico #2 on the forehead, between the ropes, and limped rapidly across the grandstand to the side of his current master.

"Hah!" said the baron, and followed that remark with several statements in a spluttering German—incomprehensible, but doubtless derogatory to the humble Enrico.

"Well, let one see," the baron said at last, his wrath cooling to a normal choler. He inspected the boots and found them irreproachable. Nevertheless, he rubbed them with a chamois boot-rubbing rag which he always kept in his pocket as a useful implement for teaching uppity stable-hands their place in the scheme of things.

"Now immediately the boots upon me place," the baron said, and thrust forth a powerful Teutonic foot.

The boot placement was accomplished after much tugging and cursing. And just in time, too, for the Mexican horseman (he had pomade on his hair!) was leaving the field to tumultuous applause.

Booted at last, with his monocle firmly set, and with his trusty horse (the famous Carnivora III by Astra out of Aspera) standing nearby, the baron marched forward to present himself to the judges.

Coming to a stop precisely three paces in front of the reviewing stand, the baron came to ramrod attention, bowed his head one-quarter of an inch, and smartly clicked his heels together.

Whereupon there was a loud explosion and a gush of gray smoke.

When the smoke had cleared away, the baron could be seen pitched forward on his face in front of the reviewing stand, as dead as last week's haddock.

Pandemonium came, followed by emotional catharsis for all of the onlookers except one lone Englishman, dressed in prebagged tweeds and Scotch-grain brogans weighing 2 and ¾ pounds apiece, who called out in a firm, loud voice, "The horse! Is the horse all right?"

Upon being assured that the baron's horse was

completely undamaged, the Englishman settled back in his seat, muttering that it was completely unfair to horses to explode explosives in their vicinity, and that in *some* countries the perpetrator of such an action would be faced with immediate police attention.

In this particular country, the perpetrator of the action also received immediate police attention. The responsible party revealed himself at once, emerging from the stable and throwing off his disguise.

Formerly he had been Enrico #1; now he stood revealed as Marcello Polletti, a man of 40, or perhaps 39, with an attractive, melancholic face, a self-deprecating smile, and a height somewhat above the middle range. He had high, prominent cheekbones suggesting deep reserves of passion, the restrained smile of the natural skeptic, and the tawny, heavy-lidded eyes which spoke strongly of a streak of indolence in the man. These qualities were immediately apparent to several thousand people in the reviewing stands, and they commented on them with pungent wisdom.

Polletti bowed gracefully to the cheering crowd and showed his Hunting license to the nearest policeman.

The policeman checked the card, punched it, saluted, and handed it back to Polletti. "Quite in order, sir. And may I be the first to congratulate you on a kill both exciting and esthetically pleasing."

"You are very kind," Marcello said.

By now he was surrounded by a crowd of reporters, thrill seekers, and well-wishers of every sort and description. The police turned back all save the genuine journalists, and Marcello answered their questions with quiet dignity.

"Why," asked a French reporter, "did you use the method of high explosive on the baron's spurs?"

"It was expedient," Polletti replied. "The man was wearing a bulletproof vest."

The journalist nodded and scribbled in his notebook, "The Prussian heel click, which has brought dread to so many, set off an ironic doom this day to one. To die in the performance of an act of symbolic arrogance—that act which presumes superior worth, which in turn presumes immortality—this must surely be called an *existential death*. Such, at least, was the view implied by Hunter Marel Poeti. . . ."

"How do you think you will make out as Victim in your next hunt?" asked a Mexican newspaperman.

"I don't really know," Marcello replied. "It will doubtless end one way or the other."

The journalist nodded and wrote down, "Mariello Polenzi killed with placidity and viewed his own imminent doom with equanimity. In this we can see the universal statement of *machismo*, that quality of manhood which engages life only through the ungrudging acceptance of death. . . ."

"Are you tough?" asked an American girl reporter.

"Definitely not," Marcello said.

She wrote, "A disinclination toward boasting, coupled with a supreme confidence in his own powers, makes Marcello Polletti a man peculiarly acceptable to American patterns of behavior. . . ."

"Are you afraid of being killed?" a Japanese reporter asked.

"Of course I am," Marcello replied.

"Zen, in at least one learned view," wrote the reporter, "is the art of seeing things as they are; Marcello Polletti, by quietly viewing his own fear of death, may be said to have conquered his own fear of death in a manner peculiarly Japanese. *Or has he?* For the question inevitably remains, is Polletti's admission of fear a magnificent conquest of the unconquerable, or a mere admission of the inadmissable?"

Polletti received a considerable amount of publicity. It wasn't every day that a man was blown up at the International Horse Show. That sort of thing made news.

And it helped, of course, that Polletti was attractive, modest, world-weary, virile, and, above all, quotable.

3

A gigantic computer clicked and chattered, flashed red lights and rippled blue ones, turned off white dots and turned on green ones. This was the games computer, the great machine which had its counterparts in all the capitols of the civilized world, and which arbitrated the destinies of all Hunters and Victims. Randomly it selected and paired the individual antagonists, recorded the results of their contest, and awarded prize money to the victor or condolences to the family of the loser, alternating the surviving players as Victim or Hunter, continuing them irrevocably in the game until one of them had reached the arbitrary limit of ten.

The rules were simple: The Hunt was open to anyone, man or woman, regardless of race, creed, or nationality, between the ages of 18 and 50. Anyone entering was in for all ten Hunts, alternately serving five as Victim and five as Hunter. Hunters received the name, address and photograph of their Victim; Victims simply received notification that a Hunter was after them. All kills had to be performed in person and there were severe penalties for killing the wrong person. Prize money was awarded in sums increasing with the number of kills. A Tens Winner, having gone the entire route successfully, was awarded almost unlimited civil, financial, political, and moral rights.

That was all there was to it. It was as easy as falling off a precipice.

There had been no more big wars since the inauguration of the Hunt; only countless millions of small ones, scaled down to the smallest possible number of contestants: two.

The Hunt was entirely voluntary, and its aim was in accord with the most practical and realistic outlook. If someone wants to kill someone, the argument ran, then why not let him try, providing we can find someone else who also wants to kill someone. That way, they can slaughter each other and leave the rest of us alone.

Though it gave the appearance of the utmost modernity, the Hunting Game was, in principle, not new at all. It was a qualitative reversion to an older, happier age when paid mercenaries did the fighting and noncombatants stayed on the sidelines and talked about the crops.

History is cyclical. An overdose of yin changes inevitably into yang. The day of the professional (and frequently nonfighting) army passed, and the age of the mass army began. Farmers could no longer talk about their crops; they had to fight for them. Even if they had no crops to fight for, they still had to fight. Factory hands found themselves involved in Byzantine intrigues in lands beyond the sea, and shoe clerks carried weapons into alien jungles and across frozen mountaintops.

Why did they do it? In those days it had all seemed very clear. Many reasons had been given, and every man adopted the rationale which suited his own particular emotionality. But what seemed obvious at the time became less so as the years passed. Professors of history argued, experts in economics demurred, psychologists begged to differ, and anthropologists felt it necessary to point out.

The farmer, shoe clerk and factory hand waited patiently for someone to tell them why they were really being killed. When no clear-cut answer was forthcoming, they became irritated, resentful, and sometimes even wrathful. Occasionally they would turn their weapons upon their own rulers.

That, of course, could not be countenanced. The growing intransigency of the people, plus the technological possibility of killing everyone and everything, definitely overloaded the yang, thereby bringing forth the yin.

After five thousand or so years of recorded history, people were finally beginning to catch on. Even rulers, notoriously the slowest of men to change, realized that something had to be done.

Wars were getting nobody nowhere; but there was still the problem of individual violence which untold years of religious coercion and police instruction had failed to curb.

The answer, for the moment, became the legalized Hunt.

That, at any rate, is one view of the growth of the institution. But it is only fair to add that not everyone agrees with this interpretation. As usual, professors of history continue to argue, experts in economics demur, psychologists beg to differ, and anthropologists feel it necessary to point out.

So, taking their objections into account, we are left with nothing but the irreducible fact of the Hunt itself; a fact as strange as the burial rites of the ancient Egyptians, as normal as the initiation ceremonies of the Sioux, and as unbelievable as the New York Stock Market.

In the final analysis, the existence of the Hunt is explicable only because of its existence; for, in at least one prominent view, *nothing* justifies the existence of *anything*.

Lights flashed, circuits clicked, relays rocked,

cam wheels rolled. Punch cards fluttered like white doves, and the games computer brought two lives together.

Hunt ACC1334BB: Hunter, Caroline Meredith. Victim, Marcello Polletti.

4

"Caroline," said Mr. Fortinbras, "I want to congratulate you on your very nice kill."

"Thank you, sir," Caroline said.

"Your ninth, I believe?"

"That is correct, sir."

"Just one more to go, mmmm?"

"Yes sir. If I make it."

"You'll make it," Fortinbras assured her. "You will make it because I, J. Walstod Fortinbras, *say* that you will make it."

Caroline smiled modestly. Fortinbras grinned immoderately. He was Caroline's boss, head of the UUU Teleplex Ampwork. He was a small man who tried to find grandeur in the grandiose, and whose taste for the vulgar was exceeded only by his enjoyment of the vile. He leaned back now, brushed the sleeve of his jacket (which was made of genuine Fulani), puffed upon a large cigar, spat upon the three-inch-thick piling of his priceless Bokhara rug, wiped his mouth with a lace handkerchief woven by indigent Brahmins beneath the burning ghats of the Ganges, and stroked his forehead with a burnished fingernail to indicate that he was thinking.

He wasn't thinking, of course; he was trying, as he had been trying for so many years, to characterize himself. The fact was, Mr. Fortinbras had no character whatsoever. Highly skilled professionals had labored for years to correct this single defect, but to no avail. This was the one great sorrow of Fortinbras' life.

"You'll be a Hunter next, hmmmm?" he asked Caroline.

"That is correct, sir."

"And you have already received notification of your next Victim?"

"I have, Mr. Fortinbras. He is a man named Marcello Polletti, a resident of Rome."

"Rome, New York?" Fortinbras asked.

"Rome, Italy," Caroline gently corrected.

"Well, all the better," Fortinbras said. "Probably more picturesque. Now my idea is this, and I want you all to think it over carefully and tell me what you really and honestly think. My idea is, since we've got a potential Tens Winner right here in our own shop, why don't we go ahead and do a documentary on her tenth kill? Hmmmm?"

Caroline nodded thoughtfully. Aside from her and Fortinbras, there were three other men in the room, all of them young, handsome, quick, talented, and obnoxious.

"Yes, *yes!*" cried Martin. As Senior Executive Assistant Producer, he was the only one (aside from Fortinbras himself) allowed to use exclamation marks.

"You've really got it, boss," Chet said softly. (To the best of his recollection, 37 documentaries had been made last year on various aspects of the Hunt.)

"Personally, I'm not so sure," said Cole. As the youngest executive assistant, it was Cole's unhappy duty to disagree with his employer, since Fortinbras would not tolerate being surrounded by yes-men. Cole hated the job, since he always felt that Fortinbras was right. He dreamed of the day when a fourth executive assistant would be hired, and he would be able to say yes.

"Three against one," Fortinbras said, disgustingly moistening the end of his cigar. "Guess you're outvoted, eh, Cole?"

"Probably just as well," Cole said cheerfully. "I feel it is my duty to state my opinions, but I can assure you that I have no faith in them."

"I like that in you," Fortinbras said. "Honesty and sound judgment can take a man a long way, make no doubt about that. Now then, let me see. Suppose we call it *The Moment of Truth.*"

Everybody concealed their winces admirably. Fortinbras said, "That, however, is merely tentative; I was just trying it on for size to see if I wanted to wear it home. What about—*The Instant of Candor?*"

"I like that very much!" Martin said instantly. "It really hits them where they live!"

"Good, good, yes, it's very good indeed," Chet said, savoring the horror of the title with half-closed eyes.

"I think it lacks something," Cole said miserably.

"*What* does it lack, precisely?" Fortinbras asked.

Cole had never before been asked to explain why he disagreed with anything. Now he felt a paralysis grip at his throat and an icy tremor pass through his stomach. These, he well knew, were sure symptoms of the onset of unemployment.

Martin, whose kind heart was proverbial as far west as Tenth Avenue, bailed him out. "I think," he said, "that what Cole had in mind was probably one of those old-fashioned punchy titles. Like calling it simply *Ten.*"

"Or perhaps he didn't have it in mind," Chet said, quickly covering for Martin.

"I think I had something or other like it in mind," Cole said, hastily covering for both of them. "But of course that short punchy stuff is sorta moldy potatoes now. . . ."

He stopped. Fortinbras, with the midfinger of his right hand pressed to a spot one inch above his vague eyebrows, was in meditation. Seconds passed. Fortinbras closed his nondescript eyes, then opened them again.

"Ten," he said in a voice barely above a whisper.

"Old timey," Martin commented. "But of course, that sort of thing comes right back into its own after a while."

"Ten," Fortinbras said, tasting the word as though it were a lollipop.

"It may have certain possibilities," Chet admitted, "though of course we must always remember—"

"TEN!" Fortinbras shouted triumphantly. "Yes, yes, TEN! It speaks to me, gentlemen, it really and truly does. Hmmmm. . . ." He took another puff on his loathsome cigar, tried unsuccessfully to twist his mouth out of shape, and said, "Has there ever been another female Tens Winner?"

"Not as far as I know," Martin replied. "Not in the United States, anyhow."

"Well, that's all we're concerned with," Fortinbras said. "We've had a few female nines, though, haven't we?"

"Miss Amelia Brandome was the last," Martin said. "She achieved nines status eight years ago." He had boned up on all this the previous night out of a prescience of the day's events. It was for this kind of thinking that Martin was a Senior Executive Assistant Producer.

"What happened to her?" Fortinbras asked.

"She got overconfident. A Victim got her on her tenth attempt. He used a shotgun filled with birdseed."

"Not a particularly *lethal*-sounding weapon," Fortinbras commented.

"Lethal enough in this case," Chet said. "The shot was delivered from a distance of approximately two inches."

"We wouldn't want you to become overconfident, Caroline," Mr. Fortinbras chuckled.

"No sir, I also wouldn't want to," Caroline said.

"Otherwise you could find yourself out of a job," Fortinbras said, in a wretched attempt at playfulness.

"I could also find myself out of a life," Caroline replied.

Everyone enjoyed Caroline's flash of wit. After the laughter had faded to a snicker, Fortinbras got down to business.

"OK, kids," he said, "Make your travel arrangements and let's get moving on this. We've got a free half hour of air time day after tomorrow, ten to ten-thirty A.M., so we'll do it then, live—or should I say dead? Heh, heh. Anyhow, you boys know the tone we want; deadly serious, but with a light touch. Don't bother with any background sequences, just get the kill in an impressive, jazzy manner, but also with humor and dignity. You know what I mean, don't you, Martin?"

"I think I can figure it out, sir," Martin said. He had been doing all of Fortinbras' thinking for three years, ever since he had become Senior Executive Assistant Producer. By next year, he figured he should be able to take over Fortinbras' position.

There could be no denying it, Fortinbras was stupid; but he was not *absolutely* stupid. He was planning to fire Martin immediately upon completion of this assignment. But that was his own little secret which he told to no one, not even his analyst.

5

The Hunt Ministry in Rome was a huge modern building in a pseudo-Romanesque style with Gothic overtones. Up its wide white steps of antiqued stone bounded Marcello Polletti, yesterday's demolisher of the Baron von Richtoffen. As he hurried upward, various sinister-looking figures dressed entirely in black detached themselves from the balustrade and surrounded him.

"Hey, mister, you wanna buy a pocket-sized metals detector?"

"It's no good against a plastic gun," Marcello said.

"As it happens," a second one said, "I got a detector for plastic, too."

Polletti smiled wanly, shrugged, and moved on.

A third man said, "Excuse me, sir, but you look like a man who could use a good spotter."

Polletti shook his head and continued up the stairs.

"But you *need* a spotter," the man insisted. "How do you expect to identify your Hunter except through the highly trained services of a spotter? Now me, I got my primary certificate in Palermo and my second-degree rating in Bologna, and I also have letters of recommendation from numerous grateful clients."

He waved a sheaf of tattered papers in Polletti's face. Polletti made murmuring sounds of regret and ducked past him. He came to the great bronze doors of the ministry, and the black-suited men slouched resignedly back to their stations along the outer balustrade.

Polletti walked down busy hallways and hurried past dusty exhibits of Hunt weapons, past world maps showing Hunt concentration points, past guided tours where badly shaven guides in tattered uniforms were lecturing on the history of the Hunt to tourists and schoolchildren. At last he reached the office he wanted.

As a bullet strikes its target, so Polletti moved in a straight, flat trajectory, and at considerable velocity, to a desk marked PAYMENTS. Behind it sat the payments clerk, a man especially chosen for his stiff, grim, uncompromising demeanor, and also for his hunched shoulders, scrawny neck and steel-rimmed spectacles.

"I've come for my prize money," said Polletti,

handing the clerk his identity card. "Perhaps you heard about how I blew up Baron Richtoffen at the horse show. It's in all the papers."

"I never read the papers," stated the clerk. "And I also do not listen to or indulge in chatter about bicycle races, soccer games, or Hunts. What did you say your name was?"

"Polletti," said Polletti, slightly crestfallen. He spelled the name for the clerk.

The clerk turned to his filing cabinet, which listed all Hunters and Victims in the Rome area. With skilled clerkish fingers he riffled the cards, and plucked out Marcello's like a chicken pecking a grain of corn.

"Yes," the clerk said at last, after examining the photograph of Polletti on the file card with the photograph of Polletti on Polletti's identity card, and then comparing both representations with the real (or allegedly real) Polletti who stood before him.

"Is everything in order?" Marcello asked.

"Quite in order," the clerk said.

"Then may I have my prize money?"

"No. It's already been claimed."

Polletti looked for a moment like a man stung by an adder. But he quickly regained his composure and asked, "Who drew it?"

"Your wife, Signora Lidia Polletti. She is your wife, is she not?"

"She was," Marcello said.

"You are divorced?"

"Annulled. Two days ago."

"It takes a week, and sometimes ten days, for changes of marital status to reach this office. You *could* lodge a complaint, of course."

The clerk smiled a smug little smile to show what he thought Marcello's chance would be of ever recovering the money.

"It is of no consequence," Marcello said, and turned and walked out. One does not show one's feelings to a clerk; but one needs money just as badly as a clerk, and probably a good deal worse. That Lidia! She could move like a rocket when money was concerned.

Outside the ministry, Marcello started to cross the street. He was rather surprised when a beautiful blonde girl ran up to him, threw her arms around his neck, and kissed him passionately. It was not the sort of thing that happened every day; and as usual, when it did happen, it was at the wrong time and he was in the wrong mood.

He began to pull away; but the girl clung to him, wailing, "Oh please, please, sir, just take me across the street and as far as the entrance of the ministry. I'll be able to take care of myself after that."

Then Marcello understood what was up. Gently he removed her hands from his neck and stepped away. "I can't help you," he told her.

"It's against the law. You see, I'm in the Hunt myself."

The beautiful blonde girl (she could have been no more than 19 or 20, or 28 at the most) watched Marcello back away, and realized that she was exposed, utterly and mercilessly, in the wide sunlit street. She turned and ran for the ministry.

A Maserati (that particular model was popularly known as The Victimizer) burst out of a side street and rushed headlong at her. The girl dodged like a matador evading a bull. But this particular bull had disc brakes, which he applied with vehemence, slewing his car to a stop in a half circle around the girl. The girl's face had hardened. From her shoulder bag she drew a bulky machine-pistol, snapped the stock out and the safeties off, and let loose a blast.

But it was sadly obvious that she had neglected to load armor-piercing bullets. Her shots glanced harmlessly off the Maserati's gleaming snout, and the driver, biding his time, leaped out the opposite side of his car and chopped her down with an antique Sten gun.

When it was all done, a policeman stepped out of the shelter of a doorway, saluted politely, and checked the Victim's card, then the Hunter's, which he punched.

"Congratulations, sir," the policeman said

formally. "Also my apologies." He handed the man a ticket.

"What's this?" the man asked.

"Traffic ticket, sir," the policeman said. He indicated the Maserati, broadside across the road and blocking traffic.

"But my dear fellow," the man said, "I could not have performed the kill without making an emergency stop."

"That is as may be," the policeman replied. "But we can make no exceptions, not even for Hunters."

"Ridiculous," the man said.

"The young lady has also broken the law," the policeman noted, "since she crossed the street against the light. But we waive the fine in her case since she is currently deceased."

"Suppose she had shot me?" the man asked.

"Then I would have fined her," the policeman said, "and I would have overlooked your traffic violation."

Polletti walked away. Squabbles over minor matters bored him almost as much as squabbles over major matters.

He had gone less than a block when a blood-red sports convertible pulled up beside him with a screech of brakes. Polletti flinched instinctively and looked around for shelter. As usual, there was none. It took him a moment to realize that the woman behind the wheel was only Olga.

She was a slim, dark, elegant young woman, exquisitely though somewhat theatrically dressed. Her eyes were large and black and very shiny, like the eyes of a jacklighted wolf. She was an extremely attractive woman if you liked the type, which could best be described as homicidal schizophrenic paranoiac with kittenish overtones.

Men like to play with danger; but not every day. Polletti had been playing with Olga for the better part of 12 years.

"I *saw*," Olga said darkly. (She always spoke darkly, except when she was speaking hysterically.)

"Saw? What did you see?"

"*Everything*," she told him.

Polletti essayed a smile. "Then if you saw everything, you surely realized that there was nothing to see."

Polletti reached out to put a hand on Olga's shoulder. Olga slipped the car into reverse and backed a few yards. Polletti dropped his hand and walked back to her. "My dear," he began again, "if you saw it all, then you surely realize that there was nothing between me and that unfortunate young lady."

"Of course not," Olga said. "Not now."

"Not now or at any other time," Polletti said.

"You must believe me, Olga, I never saw her before in my life!"

"You have lipstick on your mouth," Olga observed, darkly but with a touch of hysteria.

Polletti hastily wiped his mouth with the back of his hand. "My dear," he said, "I can assure you that between me and that unfortunate child—"

"You've always liked them young, haven't you?"

"—there was not, and had never been, anything, anything at all."

"Nothing but dreams, eh, Marcello?"

They stared at each other for some seconds. Olga was quite obviously waiting for further explanations, which she would triumphantly refute. Polletti said nothing at all. The expression on his face had changed from ritual supplication to habitual boredom. One owed something to the woman one had lived with for 12 years; something, but not this.

Abruptly he walked away from the car and began looking for a taxi. Olga slipped into gear and speeded the car straight at him, braking with only an inch or two to spare.

Without a word, Polletti got in beside her.

Olga said, "Marcello, you are a liar and a cheat."

Marcello nodded, closed his eyes, and lay back against the upholstered seat.

"If I didn't love you so much, I would kill you."

"You may yet," Polletti said, his eyes still closed.

"Quite possibly," Olga said. "But first you must see me in my new dress." She laughed and squeezed his arm. "I really think you'll like me in it, Marcello. I really think so."

"I'm sure of it," Polletti said, his eyes still closed, his head reclined on the upholstered seat.

"Why are men such pigs?" Olga asked the world at large. Receiving no answer, she slammed the car into low and took off down the street like a hurricane chased by a tornado. Polletti kept his eyes closed and engaged in several baseless fantasies.

6

A great delta-winged passenger jet circled the air high over Rome. Receiving the signal, it left the stack and came down over Fiumicino Airport. Various flaps lifted, others dropped; the jet touched down, the engines were reversed, a small tail parachute popped out, opened, and dragged a big tail parachute behind it. Brakes were applied, prayers were muttered in the pilots' compartment, and the massive aircraft came to a reluctant stop.

The doors were opened, and a mixed bag of human beings emerged. Among them was a tight little group of three homogenous men and one striking woman. A special hostess led this foursome to a nearby helicopter while the common herd were taken by bus to the airport terminal.

The four boarded. The helicopter clawed its

way into the sky and soon was over Rome. Caroline had immediately taken the seat of honor beside the pilot. Martin, Chet, and Cole were crowded into the rear seat. Martin, who had been upgraded for the duration of this one assignment to the lofty rank of Senior Production & Location Producer (Executive), was scribbling in a notebook. Chet, next in line, was chewing his lip thoughtfully. Cole, as the junior member, could do nothing but look bright and energetic.

Martin turned from his notebook and glanced down through the plexiglass floor. "Hey, isn't that St. Peter's?"

"That's it, all right," Chet said.

"You think they'd rent it to us for a day or two? Lot of ironic contrast if we got the kill there, huh?"

"I could be dressed as a nun," Caroline said dreamily.

"I'm afraid St. Peter's is out," Chet said. As Martin's Senior Executive Production Assistant, and therefore second in command, he had necessarily done a good deal of preliminary research.

"I don't mean the church," Martin said. "All we'd need is the square, with maybe a few background shots of the church itself."

"They won't let us do it," Chet said.

Cole said, "Why don't we just shoot it in a studio?"

His two seniors glared at him. "You can just

forget that idea," Martin said severely. "This is a *documentary*, remember? This is the real thing."

"Sorry," Cole said. "Hey, what's that over there?"

"Trevi Fountain," Chet said. "Pretty spot."

"Yeah," Martin said, "it *is* a pretty spot." He turned to Caroline. "What do you think, baby? You kill him there, we tilt down to show Polletti's corpse floating in the water, then reverse to show you, smiling triumphantly but with just a touch of sadness, tossing a couple of coins at him. Then we bring up the street noises hard and you walk away slowly down a long cobblestoned street and we fade out."

Chet said, "I don't think any of the streets around the Trevi Fountain are cobblestoned any more."

"So we build a cobblestoned street," Martin said impatiently, "and if they don't like it we take it down after the sequence is shot."

"It plays," Chet said judiciously. "It really plays."

"It's got class," Cole said. "It's really got class."

They all turned to Caroline. Caroline said, "No."

Martin said, "Now look—"

"Now *you* look," Caroline said. "It's my kill, my tenth kill, and I want it done big. You know what I mean, *big?* I mean really *big*."

"Big," Martin repeated. Chet chewed his lip

thoughtfully. Cole looked bright and energetic.

"That's right, *big*," Caroline stated. There was a steely note in her voice which none of them had ever heard before. Martin found her self-assurance somewhat dismaying. He didn't like it. Give a woman a few kills and she thinks she can do anything.

"There's no time for big," he explained. "We gotta shoot this thing tomorrow morning."

"That's your problem," Caroline said.

Martin reached under his sunglasses, found his eyes, and rubbed them. Working with women was tough enough; working with women killers was downright unrewarding.

Chet said, in a quiet, tentative voice, "Uh, I have a kinda idea for a location. What about we use the Colosseum? That's it down there."

The helicopter swooped low, and they all studied the massive, half-ruined oval.

"I didn't know it was so *big*," Cole said.

"I like it," Caroline said.

"Well, sure, it is pretty nice," Martin said. "But look, baby, it takes time to make arrangements for a place like this, and we haven't got much time. Wouldn't you maybe settle for the Trevi Fountain or the Borghese Gardens?"

"Here is where I will perform my kill," Caroline said implacably.

"But the arrangements—"

"Uh, Martin," Chet broke in, "it just happens

that I thought you might go for this place, so I took the liberty of taking out an option on it; you know, just in case."

"You did?"

"Yes, as a matter of fact, I did. The idea struck me late last night, and of course I didn't want to go over your head, but I also didn't want to wake you up with what was maybe just a hair-brained scheme. So I called Rome and went ahead and did it and I assure you I didn't want to go over your head or anything like that—"

"Forget it," Martin said, clapping him warmly on the shoulder. "You did just right."

"I did?" Chet asked.

"You did, and that's a fact. Caroline's satisfied, the rest of us here are satisfied, so let's get down to work. We gotta spot in our cameras and decide how to bring on the Roy Bell Dancers, and a lot of other stuff. So let's get cracking, huh, kids?"

Caroline, smiling beatifically, said, "I'm going to kill in the Colosseum! It's like some kind of a wild kid's dream come true."

"Sure it is," Martin said. "But we gotta get moving now, get everything set up, locate this Polletti and bring him in on time—"

"I'll take care of that," Caroline said.

"That's fine," Martin said. "The rest of us will have our hands full anyhow. Hey, driver, let's move!"

The helicopter swooped toward the Via Veneto. The four passengers lay back, smiling and relaxed. Martin was thinking that it was about time he got rid of Chet before Chet got rid of him. Optioning the Colosseum out from under him like that had been just a little *too* cute.

7

Polletti was walking in darkness, a complete
and utter darkness. That was bad enough. But
worse than the darkness was the complete and
abnormal silence. It was a tomblike silence—
tomblike was a very natural image for a man in
his position. He saw himself in the desolation and
quietude of incipient death, and he was fright-
ened, nervous, and bored all at the same time. He
was chewing a piece of gum and also his lower
lip, since no one could see him except through
an infrascope. His hands were loosely bent at
hip level in the ready position, an approved three
inches from his body. He moved ahead warily,
straining to receive even the faintest of sense
impressions.

Suddenly he caught the faintest glimpse of
movement, behind him and to his left—a bogie

coming toward him at 7 o'clock, one of the worst possible positions for a right-handed man.

Polletti whirled counter-clockwise, throwing himself down and to the side, out of the anticipated line of fire. This was Defensive Maneuver Three, Part 1. At the same time his right hand slapped his breast pocket. Instantly his Quickie holster slammed a gun into his hand. He could see the bogie now—a thickset, scowling man, holding a Luger at full extension. By now Polletti was prone, faced in the direction of the bogie, and firing, thus completing Part 2 of Defensive Maneuver One. He had completed the entire sequence in an incredibly short time. He felt a deep sense of exhilaration, of pleasure at a job well done. . . .

The bogie faded, overhead lights came on. Polletti was lying prone upon a dusty gymnasium floor. Ten feet in front of him was an old man wearing a soiled gray jump suit and a sour expression. The old man was seated on a stool beside a switchboard, shaking his head wearily.

"Well," Polletti asked, standing up and dusting himself off, "how did I do? I got him that time, didn't I?"

"Your reaction time," the old man said, "was nearly a tenth of a second too slow."

"I sacrificed reaction time," Polletti said warily, "in favor of precision and accuracy."

"Indeed?" said the old man.

"Yes," Polletti said. "Those are my natural aptitudes, Professor."

"Well, you can forget about them," Professor Silvestre said. "You missed the bogie by 3.2 centimeters."

"That's fairly close," Polletti said.

"But not quite close enough."

"What about my Defensive Maneuver Three?" Polletti asked. "I thought I did that rather nicely."

"Very nicely," the professor said, "and with complete and fatal predictability. A cow could have turned faster. The bogie killed you once while you were whirling, and once again when you assumed the prone position. If it had been a real Hunter, Marcello, instead of a three-dimensional projection, you would have been dead twice over."

"You're sure of that?"

"Read the dials for yourself."

"Well," Polletti said, "practice isn't like the real thing."

"Of course it isn't," the professor said, his voice mordant and inflected with a rather obvious irony. "One tends to be *slower* when it comes to the real thing. Do you remember how many times the bogie fired?"

"Twice," Polletti said promptly.

"Five times," Professor Silvestre corrected him.

"You're absolutely sure of that?"

"Read the dials. I set up the sequence myself."

"It was the echoes," Polletti said bitterly. "One can't tell the shots from the echoes in a room like this."

Professor Silvestre raised his right eyebrow all the way to where his hairline would have been, if he had had any hair. He rubbed his unshaven chin and got down from the stool. He was an ugly little gnome of a man, and not even his best friend—if he had possessed one—would have considered him entirely human. Many game instructors bore the marks of learning upon their bodies; Silvestre bore more than most. He had a stainless-steel right hand and a plastic left cheek; he also had a silver plate in his skull, a duraluminum chin, and a 14-carat gold kneecap. It was rumored that certain less visible parts of him were equally ersatz.

Psychologists have known for a long time that men who have had considerable portions of their anatomy blown up or shot away tend to become cynical. Silvestre was no exception to this rule.

"In any event," Polletti said, "I feel that I am improving. Don't you agree, Professor?"

Silvestre tried to raise his right eyebrow, but found that it was already raised as far as it would go. Therefore he lowered it and closed his left eye completely. He seemed about to speak; then stopped, reserving judgment.

"Come," he said briskly, "we will proceed to the next examination."

He pressed a button on his switchboard. A panel opened and a miniature bar shot out of the wall and stopped with such force that half a dozen champagne glasses were thrown into the air. Polletti winced as they smashed against the floor.

"I told the mechanic to do something about the recoil," Professor Silvestre said. "You get nothing these days but shoddy workmanship. Come, Polletti, we will proceed with the examination."

Deftly the professor mixed a drink from several unmarked bottles and handed it to Polletti.

Polletti sniffed cautiously, frowned judiciously, and said, "Gin and angostura, with just a trace of tabasco."

Without a word the professor mixed and handed him another drink.

"Vodka, lemon and milk," Polletti declared, "and just a hint of tarragon vinegar."

"You're sure?" the professor asked.

"Quite sure," said Polletti.

"Drink some, then."

Polletti lifted the drink, looked at Silvestre, sniffed, frowned, and put the drink down.

"I think I would prefer not to drink it," he said.

"Just as well," Silvestre said. "As it happens,

that was not a trace of vinegar you smelled; it was a sizable amount of arsenic."

Polletti smiled with embarrassment and found that he was shuffling his feet like a schoolboy. He stopped shuffling and said, "I have a head cold today. You could hardly expect. . . ."

One look from the professor was enough to silence him. Silvestre pushed a button on his switchboard. A sofa shot out from the wall, nearly taking the wall with it as it came to a jolting stop. Both men sat down.

After a short but pregnant silence, Silvestre said: "Marcello, up to now you have lived a charmed life."

"Isn't that true of all men?" Polletti asked quickly. "I mean to say, when one considers the fortuitous and inexplicable nature of life itself—"

The professor was not to be put off. Inexorably he continued: "On your first time out you had the good fortune to be selected for Hunter, and you were matched against a feebleminded Englishman."

"He wasn't feebleminded," Polletti said. "He was just rather set in his ways."

"He was a pushover," Silvestre continued, "a Hunter's dream. Next you were a Victim, but your assigned Hunter was a 19-year-old suffering from an unsuccessful love affair. Again, the kill was simplicity itself; as a matter of fact, I suspect that the poor boy was simply looking for a socially approved means of suicide."

"Nothing of the sort," Polletti said. "He was merely a little absentminded."

"And the third time you were a Hunter, and you drew that ridiculous German baron who could think of nothing but horses."

"He *was* rather easy," Polletti admitted.

"They were all easy!" Silvestre cried. "But how long do you think it can go on like that? Have you ever considered the law of averages? You haven't come up against one competent antagonist yet! How much longer do you think it can go on like that? Do you honestly believe you can get by without brains, quick thinking, intuition, and intensive training?"

"Now look," Polletti said. "I'm not as bad as all that. I've been a Victim in my fourth Hunt for nearly twenty-four hours, and absolutely nothing has happened."

"You're probably being stalked," Silvestre said. "Your Hunter is undoubtedly sizing you up, establishing the pattern of your movements, waiting for the moment of maximum opportunity in which to strike. And you aren't even aware of it."

"I doubt that very much," Polletti said, with quiet dignity.

"Do you indeed? Let's see how you do on identification."

Professor Silvestre pressed a button on his switchboard. The room went black. He pressed another button. Five life-sized figures appeared on the far side of the room. Four of the figures in this particular test were harmless; "angels" in Hunt terminology, which had borrowed many expressions from the legendary World War II. One was a bogie. It was Polletti's job to identify the disguised killer.

Polletti looked at the figures with care. They were dressed as a policeman, a Swissair hostess, a Jesuit priest, a hotel porter, and a Jordani Arab. They walked slowly toward the couch and then disappeared.

Silvestre turned on the lights. "Well? Which was the Hunter?"

"Could I see them again?" Polletti asked.

Silvestre shook his head. "I gave you an additional second as it was."

Marcello rubbed his chin, ruffled his hair, and said, "That Arab didn't look exactly right. . . ."

"Wrong," Silvestre said. He pressed a button and the Jesuit priest appeared alone, somewhat ghostlike since the room lights were on, but clearly visible.

"Observe," Silvestre said. "The Jesuit is an unmistakable fraud. He has the 'J' of his order on the right breast as well as on the left—a clear giveaway!"

"I've never paid much attention to Jesuits,"

Polletti said, standing up and rattling the small change in his pocket.

"Rome is swarming with them!" Silvestre said.

"Exactly why I've never noticed them."

"But that's exactly why you *must* notice them!" Silvestre cried. "The off-key detail in the commonplace is the surest clue of all." He shook his head sadly. "When I was in the Hunt, one paid real attention to such things. Nothing ever escaped my observation."

"Nothing but that explosive banana," Polletti said.

"True," Silvestre admitted. "That Nigerian fellow found out about my weakness for tropical fruit."

"And I believe there were a few other mishaps," Polletti reminded him.

"I am quite aware of it," Silvestre said with dignity. "Luck always ran against me, and now I try to teach others to avoid my own failures. I've had some notable successes. But I don't think I can count you among them, Marcello."

"Perhaps not," Polletti said carelessly.

"You have been through my entire course," Silvestre said. "And you are not totally lacking in native ability. But there is something about you —some basic core of indifference, something that renders you incapable of putting your heart and soul into man's noblest occupation—murder!"

"I suppose that's true," Polletti said. "I simply can't seem to stay interested long enough."

"I fear you have a serious character defect," Professor Silvestre said gravely. "My boy, what will become of you?"

"I suppose that I'll die," Marcello said.

"Probably," Silvestre agreed. "But more important than that is the question of *how* you will die. Are you going to die magnificently, like a kamikaze, or miserably, like a cornered rabbit?"

"I can't see that it makes much difference," Polletti said.

"It makes *all* the difference!" the professor cried. "If you cannot kill well, then at least you ought to die well. Otherwise you will bring discredit upon your family, your friends, and upon Professor Silvestre's School for Victim Tactics. Remember our slogan here: 'Die as Well as You Kill.'"

"I'll try to bear it in mind," Polletti said, getting to his feet.

"My boy, my boy," Silvestre said, rising and resting his stainless-steel hand on Polletti's shoulder, "your apparent indifference is but a mask for your essential masochism. You must try to fight, not only the deadly Hunter outside, but the even deadlier antagonist within your own mind."

"I'll try," Polletti said, trying to suppress a yawn. "But just now I have an appointment—"

"Of course, of course," the professor said. "But first there is the little matter of my bill, which we might as well settle now. Today brings it to 300,000 lire. If you could—"

"I can't just at the moment," Polletti said, becoming aware that the professor's stainless-steel hand was about an inch from his left carotid artery. "But first thing tomorrow, as soon as the banks open, I'll have it for you."

"You could write me a check," Silvestre suggested.

"Unfortunately, I have no checks on me."

"Luckily," the professor said, "I do."

"Sadly," Polletti said, "I can't write a check at the moment since my funds are in a safe-deposit box."

Silvestre looked hard at his unpromising pupil, then shrugged and took his steel hand away from Polletti's neck.

"Very well," he said. "Tomorrow, on your word of honor?"

"On my word of honor," Polletti said.

"Let's shake on it," the professor said, extending his steel hand.

"I think I'd rather not," Polletti said.

The professor smiled and offered his good left hand. Polletti shook it warmly. Silvestre pulled his hand back convulsively and gazed at the palm. In the center of it there was a single drop of blood.

"Do you see?" Marcello said, showing the glittering little spike affixed to the palm of his hand. "As you pointed out, the off-key detail within the commonplace. Now if I had dipped that spike in curare. . . ."

Chuckling with good nature, he walked to the door.

Silvestre sat down, sucking his pierced palm. He felt unhappy. Despite his frivolous tricks, Marcello Polletti was surely headed for a grave-yard. But then, he reminded himself, so were all men; whereas he, Professor Silvestre, was probably headed for a junk heap.

8

In the Borgia Ballroom of the Rome Hilton, Caroline was rehearsing her post-kill dance number with the Roy Bell Dancers. There was utter silence except for an occasional exclamation, such as: "I told you the *pink spotlight*, you mindless, incompetent moron, not the white overheads!"

Martin, Chet, and Cole sat in the front row of the hastily erected little theater, pinching their upper lips judiciously. They could see that Caroline was no Pavlova; but then she didn't have to be a Pavlova. What she lacked in dancing ability (which was considerable) she made up for in sheer female magnetism (which was more than considerable). The Roy Bell Dancers skillfully portrayed the various aspects of Woman; but Caroline had no need to portray—she *was* Woman. Sometimes she made you think of a vampire, sometimes of a Valkyrie. Her tall, lithe body seemed incapable of an awkward gesture, and her long blonde hair streamed down her shoulders like a perilous bright flag of promise.

"She's not much of a dancer," Martin said, still pinching his upper lip, "but she's all Woman."

Chet nodded. "It's amazing. Sometimes she makes you think of a vampire, sometimes of a Valkyrie."

"That's for sure," said young Cole, removing his fingers from his upper lip. "And have you noticed how her tall, lithe body seems incapable of making an awkward gesture, and how her long blonde hair streams down her shoulders like a bright perilous flag of promise?"

"Shaddap," Martin said, still pinching his upper lip. He had been on the verge of saying that himself, and he hated to have underlings snatch the words right out of his mouth. He decided to have Cole fired along with Chet. Martin hated a wise guy.

The dance came to an end. Panting slightly but deliciously, Caroline left the stage and flung herself into a seat next to Martin.

"Well?" she asked. "How was I?"

The three men made noises of approval, the loudest and most definite coming from Martin, due to his seniority.

"And everything is set up at the Colosseum for tomorrow morning?" she asked.

"The works," Martin assured her. "Lights, stages, remote-control microphones, five active cameras and two more on standby. We've even got a special narrow-beam shotgun mike so we can pick up the Victim's death rattle."

"Sounds OK," Caroline said. She mused for a moment, and her protean face, formerly that of vampire or Valkyrie, changed into that of Diana, the implacable maiden huntress. "Now, let's see some stills of this Polletti."

Martin gave her a batch of shiny 8 x 10 photographs of Polletti, shot earlier that day and developed, processed, enlarged, and delivered in a matter of hours, due to the miracle of money.

Caroline studied the pictures closely. Abruptly she asked, "How old is this guy?"

"About forty," Martin said.

"And what sign was he born under?"

"Gemini," Chet answered promptly.

"Untrustworthy," Caroline declared. "Especially with those crinkles around the eyes."

"I think he was squinting when our man took the pictures," Cole said timidly.

"A crinkle is a crinkle," Caroline declared. "But I like his hands. Did you notice? He's got spatulate fingers, except for the left ring finger."

"You're right," Martin said. "I didn't even notice before."

"I don't suppose you got a phrenologist's report on him?"

"Gee, Miss Caroline," Cole said, "there just wasn't time."

"What difference does it make what bumps he has on his head?" Martin asked. "All you got to do is kill the guy, Caroline."

"I like to know something about the people I kill," Caroline said. "It makes it nicer, somehow."

Martin shook his head with exasperation. That was just like a woman; always dragging in the personal element. He decided to fire Caroline as soon as he had taken over Fortinbras' job; then, with a slight start of dismay, he realized that after her tenth kill, Caroline would be in an excellent position to have *him* fired.

"I know what you mean," Martin said, hastily transforming his exasperation at her into anger at himself. "It *is* nicer to know, and if there had been any possible way of getting a phrenologist's report on Polletti, Chet would surely have figured out a way."

Caroline seemed about to say something— probably caustic, to judge from the shape of her mouth; but she was interrupted by a tinny voice from a small monitor nestling comfortably at Chet's feet.

"Hello, hello," the voice from the monitor said. "This is Mobile Camera 3, proceeding approximately south-southwest and a point west along the Via Giulia. Do you read me, Central Command Post, do you read me?"

"Yeah, we hear you okay," Martin said. (He hated stuffy formalities almost as much as he hated egalitarian informalities.)

"I have the Target presently in view at a range of approximately thirty-seven and four-tenths feet. Do you wish me to effect a maximum closure, or shall I open up at present range, interrogative."

"*Open up?*" Caroline cried. "Just whose hunt does he think this is?"

"He doesn't mean to shoot," Martin explained. "He just wants to know if he should televise from his present range or move in closer. I can't bear these former destroyer captains, but Fortinbras hires them by the boatload." He turned a switch on the monitor. "Hold your position, Mobile 3, and by no means—repeat, *by no means*—move in any closer. Give us what you've got."

"Affirmative," the voice from the monitor said, so briskly that you could almost see his bristling ginger moustache.

The gray face of the monitor turned white, then red with jagged green and crimson lines. At last the picture cleared and showed a lovely sad lady staring with downcast eyes (no mean feat) at three moustached men with compressed lips. A voice said in Italian, "And today we bring you a further episode in the strange, tangled lives of—"

Chet shouted, "Hey, Mobile 3, get on the ball!"

"Aye, sir," Mobile 3 replied. "Sorry, sir. Little mixup in the omnidirectional pickup."

"Is that meant to be an excuse?" Martin asked ominously.

"No, sir. Merely an explanation. Here we go, sir."

The screen went blank, then came to life again. Marcello Polletti was clearly visible now, walking down a street. His shoulders were slumped and his step was listless.

"All the earmarks of a chronic depressive," Chet said at once.

"Maybe he's just tired," Caroline suggested, studying Polletti's image with care.

"He looks like an ideal Victim type," Cole said, with boyish enthusiasm.

"The only ideal Victim is a dead Victim," Caroline said coldly. "I think he's lazy."

"Is that good?" young Cole asked hopefully.

"No, it's bad," Caroline told him. "You can't tell what the lazy ones are apt to try." She studied Polletti for a few more seconds. "But there's something else, something more than laziness, or depression, or tiredness. He's not hiding or evading or any of the stuff a Victim is supposed to do. He's just walking along a public street, a perfect target."

"It does seem sorta odd," Martin admitted.

"Are you sure he's been officially notified?"

"I'll check it out," Martin said masterfully. He

clicked his fingers; Chet waved two fingers impatiently; Cole hurried to the rear, found a telephone, and plugged it in.

Martin dialed the Hunt Ministry in Rome, tried to make his English understood through a torrent of Italian, and turned helplessly to his assistants.

"Uh, chief," Chet said, "I took a one-night hypnosomnic course in Italian, just to be on the safe side. So if you'd like—"

Martin handed over the telephone. Speaking in a flawless Florentine accent, Chet learned that B.27.38 Polletti, Marcello, had indeed received personal and official notification of his current Victim status in a Hunt.

"Weird," Martin commented. "Definitely weird. Where's he going now?"

"Into a house," Caroline said. "Did you think he'd walk the streets the rest of the day for the benefit of your camera crews?"

They watched Polletti walk through a doorway. After that, the monitor showed nothing but a closed door.

Martin pressed a button on the monitor. "All right, Mobile 3. The Target is out of view, so you can go to black. Are you able to keep the Target's house under surveillance for an hour or two without arousing suspicion?"

"Affirmative," the voice from the monitor crackled back. "I am operating from the rear of a

Volkswagen. So far, to the best of my knowledge, no one has even looked at me."

"Nice going," Martin said. "What's the address of that house? Right, got it. We will relieve you in about an hour, two at the most. You will stay in the car; if you think you are arousing any suspicion, drive away immediately. Okay?"

"Wilco," the cameraman said.

"See you later," Martin said.

"Over and out," the cameraman responded.

Martin punched the button and turned to Caroline. "Well, sweetie, we found the guy, and we also found out where he lives. It is now 3:34 P.M. and 15 seconds. You have to get him into the Colosseum by tomorrow morning. It's not the easiest job in the world. Think you can bring it off?"

"I think I can," Caroline said in dulcet tones. "Do *you* think I can?"

Martin looked at her, then defensively pinched his upper lip. "Yeah," he said, "I guess maybe I really think you can. Caroline, you've changed."

"I know," Caroline said. "Perhaps it's the influence of Rome, or of my tenth kill, or both. Or maybe it's something else. I'll be in touch with you, boys."

She turned and walked magnificently out of the Borgia Ballroom.

9

Marcello Polletti's apartment had a bright, chic, impermanent look, as had Polletti himself. The furniture was low, comfortable, harmonious, and pleasing to the eye—although, like its master, it was of no particular period or style, and of dubious intrinsic worth. There were three interior stairways; one led to a terrace, another to a bedroom, and the third, not yet having found a destination, ended in a blank white wall. This, to strain an already overdrawn analogy, was equally symbolic of Polletti.

Polletti himself was stretched out on a dapper crimson couch. He had a little red and blue toy monkey on his chest (transistorized; rechargeable battery; five-year guarantee; fully washable; fun for the entire family!). He scratched it absent-mindedly behind the ear and the pseudosimian twitched and chattered. He stopped scratching and started to practice deep breathing. But after three inhalation-exhalation cycles he gave it up because, like so many other things, it made him dizzy and faintly nauseous. Besides, he knew that he was doing quite well just to be breathing at all. In his circumstances, deep breathing was presumptuous, since it rested upon the illusion of a length of time in which to breathe.

He smiled faintly; he had made an aphorism, or possibly an apothegm.

On the wall opposite him was a television set resting in a wall bracket. Beside him was a low coffee table containing six books, a newspaper, 15 comic books, one bottle of whiskey, two unwashed glasses, one aluminum-framed Smith and Wesson (Model XCB3, known as The Retaliator), fully loaded but lacking a firing pin. (He had been planning to have it fixed.) The coffee table also contained a clever little one-shot derringer with a total length of 1.2 inches, perfect for concealment and reasonably accurate at distances up to three feet. Beside the derringer were two other hand guns of dubious lineage and doubtful ability. Draped across the southeast corner of the table was a bulletproof vest, the latest model, manufactured two years ago by Hightree & Ouldie, Bulletproof Vestmakers by Appointment to Her Majesty, the Queen. The vest weighed 20 pounds and would stop any cartridge load except the new Super Penetrex 9 mm Magnum developed last year by Marshlands of Fiddler's Court, Bulletmakers by Appointment to His Majesty, the King. The Super Penetrex was now the standard load for all Hunters.

Near the vest were three crumpled cigarette packs and one half-full pack of Régies. And finally, there was a half-finished cup of coffee on the coffee table.

The television set, pretimed, turned itself on. It was The Hunt Hour International, a program one simply had to watch in order to know who was being killed by whom, and how.

Today's show was being telecast from Dallas, Texas, a city with more game birds (as they were affectionately called) per capita than any other metropolis in the world. For this reason Dallas was known as Homicide Heaven, and was a sort of Mecca for aficionados of violence.

The announcer was a mild, friendly looking young American, who spoke in that mixture of natural friendliness and easy familiarity which is so difficult to simulate and so easy to dislike.

"Hi there, folks," he said, "and a very special hi to all the aggressive young boys and girls out there who'll be the Hunters and Victims of the future. I have a special message for you kids, because a special matter has been brought to my attention. So without moralizing, kids, I'd just like to remind you that it's morally wrong to kill your parents even if you've got what seems like a good reason; and it's also against the law. So really, and I'm very serious about this, kids, *don't do it*. Go see your gym instructor and he'll arrange a fight for you with someone your own size and weight, using truncheon, cestus, or mace, depending upon your age and scholastic standing. I know it's not the real thing; I know a lot of you kids think that a few broken bones or a concussion is pretty mild stuff. But believe me, it's good clean sport, it helps to build healthy bodies and develop quick reflexes, and it really knocks out those old aggressions. I know that a lot of you kids out there think a gun or a grenade is the only thing that really counts; but that's because you've never fooled around with anything else. And let me just remind you of this: the ancient Roman gladiators used the cestus, and nobody thought *they* were sissies. The knights of the feudal ages swung a pretty mean mace, and nobody laughed at *them*. So how about it, huh, kids? How about giving it a try?"

Polletti murmured to himself, "I wish I were a child again."

"You are," a sepulchral voice said from the top of the second staircase.

Polletti didn't look up; it was only Olga, moving silently down from the bedroom.

"And here are some other news and views from the World of the Hunt," the announcer was saying. "In India, a recent but widespread revival of the ancient cult of thuggee has been officially confirmed by the Foreign Office at New Delhi. A spokesman for the government said today—"

"Marcello," said Olga.

Polletti waved one hand impatiently. The television screen was showing stock footage of Bombay.

"—that thuggee, the ages-old practice of strangulation by means of a silk sash, or, in cases of extreme poverty, by a cotton sash—"

"Marcello," Olga said again, "I am so sorry." She had come halfway down the staircase, leaning heavily on the bannister for support.

"—is one of the few forms of murder readily available to people in all walks of life which does not break the commandment, explicitly stated in many of the world's great religions, against the shedding of blood. Various Buddhist groups in Burma and Ceylon have expressed interest in this concept, which a spokesman for the Kremlin has called—and I quote—'sheerest casuistry.' This view was challenged, however, by a spokesman for the Chinese People's Government, who is quoted by the New China Agency as having hailed the thuggee sash (or the Tsingtao Neck Covering, as he called it) as a true People's Weapon and therefore—"

"Marcello!"

Polletti turned his head reluctantly and saw

that Olga had reached the bottom of the staircase. Medusalike, her unbound black hair fell to her shoulders in snaky ringlets; her mouth was painted crimson and squared at the sides in the new "pythoness" fashion; and her great black obelisk eyes had become unfocused and dull, like the hopeless eyes of a jacklighted wolf who has been shot in the gut.

"Marcello," she asked, "can you ever forgive me?"

"Of course," Polletti said promptly, and turned back to the television set.

"Meanwhile, President-elect Gilberte of Brazil opened Section 2 of the World Olympics with a solemn statement. He told the millions packed into the Rio Central Stadium that primary emotional catharsis, as canalized and directed in the Hunt, was not yet economically possible for all; whereas the Olympic Gladiatorials, which gave the finest and most powerful form of secondary emotional catharsis available, were within the means of every citizen. He further stated that attendance at the games was the duty of every citizen who sincerely wished to avert the massed-slaughter warfare of the past. His words were greeted with respectful applause. The first contest today was between Antonio Abruzzi, three-time European champion of the free-style Battle-ax Event, against the popular Finnish left-hander Aesir Drngi, victor at last year's North European semifinals. An upset seemed in the making when—"

"I was driven to it," Olga said. Her knees began to buckle and her whitened grip on the banister came loose. "I am sorry, Marcello—so very, very sorry." The banister slipped away from her straining right hand. Her left hand opened as of its own volition, and from it fell an ominous brown bottle of sinister shape and obvious intent. Polletti recognized it at once; it was the bottle in which Olga kept her sleeping pills—or in which she used to keep her sleeping pills, for the brown bottle was unstoppered and rolled emptily across the floor.

It was clear to anyone that Morpheus had formed a fatal alliance with his brother Thanatos.

"I took an overdose of sleeping pills," Olga said, in case it was not clear to Marcello. "I sup-pose—I suppose—" Here words failed her, and the wretched girl crumpled onto the taupe rug.

"—while in the Broadsword Competition, Nicholai Groupopolis of Greece scored a clear first, delivering the death stroke with an upward-slanting backswing against Edouard Comte-Couchet of France, his gallant but clearly out-classed rival. In Middleweight Strangulation, a surprise upset was scored by Kim Sil Kul of the Republic of Central Korea."

"Excuse me," Polletti said, looking up guiltily

from the screen. "Did you say you were having trouble sleeping?"

"In the Class B Double Stiletto Classic, a draw was proclaimed between Juanito Rivera of Oaxaca, Mexico, and Giulio Carerri of Palermo, Sicily, while in—"

"I said," Olga said in a weak but distinct voice, "that I took an overdose of sleeping pills; of *barbiturates*, to be more precise."

"—the Grenade-throwing Event, Middleweight Division, Michael Bornstein of Omaha, Nebraska, despite a shoulder separation, blew his opponent—"

"And furthermore," Olga said, "I have no regrets, except for *you*, Marcello, since it is you who have driven me to this by your indifference over the last twelve years, and it is you who, if there is a vestige of conscience somewhere within your callous soul, will suffer worse pangs than I am suffering now, and will someday come to realize that inaction is a warped form of action and that inattention is a perverted form of attention; and when that day comes—"

"Olga," Polletti said.

"Yes?" Olga said, her voice barely audible above her Cheyne-Stokes breathing.

"I forgot to refill your sleeping-pill prescription the other day."

Olga rose gracefully to her feet, found cigarettes on a nearby table and lighted one. She inhaled deeply, blew smoke at the ceiling, and said, "Marcello, why don't you ever do anything for me? You were passing right by the drugstore yesterday."

Polletti wrinkled his forehead. He had always admired Olga's refusal to allow any embarrassing situation to embarrass her.

"—and in the special Armored-car Event, an Aston-Martin Vulcan V scored an extremely accurate—or extremely lucky—first hit on a favored Mercedes-Benz Death's Head 32."

Olga walked over to a vase of artificial roses, which she rearranged hideously with a few light, deft motions. She did nearly everything with style, even if she did nearly everything wrong.

"Marcello," she said, in the light, playful voice which she reserved for the most serious matters, "why don't we get married? It would be such fun—it really would, Marcello."

"I am already married," Polletti said.

"But if you weren't?"

"Then we could consider the question in a much more realistic way," Polletti replied, with the automatic caution one acquires after 12 years with the same mistress.

Olga smiled sadly and started up the terrace staircase. Near the top she turned and said, "I don't believe you *are* married any more. Your annulment has come through, hasn't it, Marcello?"

"Unfortunately, it hasn't," Polletti replied, in

the grave, straightforward, manly tone he reserved for his most serious lies. "One can't rush the authorities in these matters. For all I know, it'll never come through."

"It has! Admit it!"

Marcello turned away from her and played with his little electronic monkey. It reminded him of himself. The television screen was showing a third-round elimination melee: six men to a side, regulation rapiers, leather armor. The Spaniards seemed to be getting the better of the Germans in this contest.

Olga took one more step up the staircase and came to a heavy terra cotta vase she had put there the previous day. The sight of it, and of the recumbent, complacent Polletti infuriated her. "Beast! Swine! Ox!" she shouted. She picked up the vase, tottered for a moment under its weight, then threw it.

Polletti didn't bother to move. The vase missed his head by an inch or two, shattering on the floor. Poor Olga always missed: targets, true love, husbands, parties, luncheon appointments, sessions with her analyst—anything you cared to name. Dr. Hoffhauer had told her that she was an extreme masochist who tried to compensate for her self-destructive urges through the acting out of pseudospontaneous sadistic impulses which, of course, her overdeveloped death wish would never allow her to accomplish. That was very bad. But, the doctor had pointed out, Polletti was in even worse shape (judging by what she said about him), since his death wish seemed to have no ameliorating sadistic impulses to help hold it in line.

The Hunt Hour International ended, and the television set turned itself off. Polletti, calm possessor of a hypothetical uncompensated death wish, rose to his feet, brushed terra cotta dust out of his hair, and started toward the door.

"Where are you going?" Olga asked accusingly.

"Out," Polletti said mildly.

"Out *where?*"

"Just out."

"Then take me with you."

"I can't," Polletti said. "I'm going to the Hunt Club. They allow only accredited Hunters or Victims."

"They allow everybody!"

"Not to the Members' Annex #1," Polletti said. "And that's where I'm really going."

"But you said before that you were just going out."

"I am just going out," Polletti said. "But *after* I've just gone out, I'm going to the Hunt Club."

"Pig!" Olga shouted.

"Oink," Polletti replied, and walked out the door.

10

"This is Mobile One to Central. Do you read me, Central, do you read me? Over."

"I read you loud and clear," Martin said. He was Central. Almost the first thing he had done upon his arrival in Rome was to organize a command post. That was something he had always wanted—a command post with himself in charge under the code name of Central. He had it now; and he also had about $200,000 worth of radio and television equipment in one corner of the Borgia Ballroom. He was sitting in front of his equipment with a microphone in one hand and a cigarette in the other. He was also wearing earphones. This pleased him very much.

"This is Mobile Two reporting. But I have nothing to report."

"Then carry on as before," Martin said firmly.

The Roy Bell Dancers, having finished another

rehearsal, were lounging on the stage, drinking black coffee and discussing ways to keep one's fingernails from splitting. Caroline had been reading a book on the care and raising of cocker spaniels. Now she put the book down and strolled to Martin's command post.

"Mobile Three signing in."

"*Reporting* in, you mean," Martin corrected him.

"Sorry. Mobile Three reporting in with nothing to report in."

"Acknowledged," Martin said curtly, taking a drag from his cigarette, wiping his forehead and pinching his lip. The earphones hurt his ears but he wasn't going to take them off for a small matter like that. He could endure the pain; he knew that other men had probably endured worse.

"Mobile Four reporting. Hey look, Martin, what about if—"

"Not *Martin*," Martin said reprovingly. "*Central* is the correct nomenclature in this situation." Martin shook his head with annoyance. That was Chet in Mobile Four. He was probably annoyed at having to work as a spotter, and as fourth spotter at that. But that was just the way it had happened to turn out, which was how things did happen to turn out sometimes. And anyhow, Chet shouldn't presume on their 12-year friendship to the extent of using Martin's first name— not after Martin had explained to everybody the need for radio code integrity in an operation of this sort.

"Your report, Mobile Four," Martin barked.

"Nothing to report, Central," Chet said. "Mobile Four requests permission to take a lunch break."

"Negative," Martin replied.

"Now look, Central, I didn't have any time for breakfast—"

"But you *did* have time to rent the Colosseum," Martin said.

"Now look, I explained about that. I really didn't mean to—"

"*Request denied!*" Martin howled. In a calmer voice he added, "I got a feeling something's going to pop at any moment now. Can't spare you just now, Mobile Four; I really can't."

"So okay," Mobile Four, or Chet, replied. "I shall maintain surveillance until ordered otherwise. Out and over. I mean over and out."

Martin gripped the microphone convulsively. Lord, lord, how he hated levity, slackness, presumption, insubordination, and other things like that! He hadn't realized how much he hated those things until today, when he was finally in charge of his own operation. He could almost feel a vestige of sympathy for Mr. Fortinbras.

"Gee, you've certainly got a lot of equipment there," Caroline said, in a voice which indicated her complete lack of interest.

"We've got what we need," Martin said. "You can't run an operation like this on two tin cans and a piece of string." He tried to draw toughly on his cigarette but found that he had crushed it earlier, while convulsively gripping the microphone. He lit another cigarette and drew on it toughly.

"What's that little dial all the way over on the far left?" Caroline asked.

Martin hadn't the faintest idea, but he replied promptly, "That's the multiphase variable overload rheostat component."

"Gee," said Caroline. "Is it important?"

Martin smiled tightly and drew toughly on his cigarette. "Important?" This whole jury-rigged switchboard would probably blow itself to bits without the MPVORC. So I guess you could maybe call it important."

"Why would it blow itself to bits?" Caroline asked.

"Well, it's mainly because of the line voltage input resonance factor," Martin told her. "It's sort of an interesting phenomenon, actually. I could explain the whole thing to you if you're interested."

"Never mind," Caroline said.

Martin nodded. Sometimes he felt he could conquer the world.

"This is Mobile One!" a voice screamed in his

earphones. "The Target is just leaving his house! Repeat, the Target—"

"I got it the first time," Martin said. "And don't shout into that microphone, you wanna deafen me?"

"Sorry, Central. I guess I was keyed up after these hours of waiting."

"So okay, forget it. Any other units got him?"

"Mobile Four reporting. I've got him."

"Mobile Three reporting. Target not yet in line of sight."

"Mobile Two reporting with same message."

"*Which* same message?" Martin roared.

"The same message as Mobile Three. I mean, I can't see the Target."

"That's okay," Martin said. "Mobiles Two and Three, hold your positions. Mobile One, I want you to—"

"CQ, CQ, calling CQ," a high clear voice said into Martin's earphones. It was a voice Martin had never heard before, and he immediately suspected espionage, counterespionage, and various other things.

"Huh?" he replied, promptly but noncommittally.

"Hi there," said the voice. "This is 32ZOZ-4321, Bob's the handle, I'm thirteen years old and I'm DX'ing out of Wellington, New Zealand, on a rebuilt Hammarlund 3BBC21 utilizing an eighty-foot power-driven dummy-load Arcana aerial with a surplus Dormeister for narrow-beam stratobounce redaction. I'm willing to talk to any of my brother hams, though I'm looking especially for ham operators in Cairo, Bokhara, and Mukden, with whom I'd like to exchange DX cards and general gossip. How do you read me? I've been having a little trouble with the Dormeister lately, but I think maybe it's just sunspots. Over."

"Get off the air!" Martin bellowed.

"I've got just as much right on the air as you have," replied 32ZOZ4321 with dignity.

"You're on a privately assigned commercial frequency!" Martin said. "You are jamming me at a crucial moment. Over."

There was a brief silence. Then 32ZOZ4321 said, "Gosh, mister, you're right! My 3BBC21 is a great little rig, but it does drift a little. But that's mainly because I haven't been able to afford the right parts so I can really lock on. I'm terribly sorry, mister, I really am. Over."

"Forget it; I was young once myself, kid. Now will you please get off my frequency? Over."

"I'm going right off. Gee, mister, I hope you don't report this. I could lose my license. Over."

"I won't report it if you'll *get off the air right now. Over!*"

"I'm going right off and thanks a lot, mister. Would you mind telling me how my signal was? Over."

"Five by five. Over," Martin replied.

"Thank you, sir. Over and out."

"Over and out," Martin repeated.

"Over and out," Mobile One said promptly.

"No, not you!" Martin said.

"But you said—"

"Never mind what I said. What about the Target?"

"I have him in sight," Mobile One said. "He is proceeding along the Via Cavour and has just reached the intersection of the Via dei Fori Imperiali. He has paused, and— Damn. A bus just interposed between me and the Target."

"Mobile Four reporting," Chet said. "I've got him. He's still standing on the corner. The Target's hands are in his pockets and his shoulders are slumped. He is looking upward now, looking rather intently—"

"At what?" Martin cried.

"A cloud," Mobile Four stated. "It's the only thing up there."

"Why would he be looking at a cloud?" Martin asked Caroline.

"Maybe he likes clouds," Caroline said.

"Mobile Three reporting. I've got him, Central! Target is proceeding along a street with an illegible name, moving north-northwest and a point west on an intersection course with the Forum of Trajan, which was designed by Apollodorus of Damascus and is still in remarkably good shape after eighteen hundred years of various vicissitudes."

"Just give me the relevant information, please, Mobile Three," Martin said. "But I like your spirit."

"Mobile Three reporting. I've got him! That illegible street is the Via Quattro Novembre. The Target has now come to a complete stop approximately thirty-seven yards south of Santa Maria di Loreto."

"Acknowledged," Martin said. Whirling around to a huge wall map of Rome and its environs, he marked Polletti's progress on an acetate overlay. He drew a thick black line for confirmed movements and a dotted red line for probable advances.

"Mobile One reporting. I've got him. He's still stopped."

"What's he doing?" Martin asked.

"I think he's scratching his nose," Mobile One said.

"You'd better be sure of that," Martin said ominously.

"Mobile Two reporting with confirmation of Mobile One's report. The Target, as seen through Zeiss 8 X 50 tripod-mounted binoculars, *is* scratching his nose. . . . Correction. Target has just terminated the preceding action."

"Mobile Two reporting. Target is moving again, proceeding in a general northerly direction along the Via Pessina to the intersection of the Via Salvatore Tommasi."

Martin turned to his map, glared, squinted, then turned back to the microphone. "I can't find those streets, Mobile Two. Let me have them again."

"Roger. Target is proceeding. . . . Sorry, Central, somebody must have given me the wrong map inset. Those last streets I gave you are in Naples. I don't know how it could have happened—"

"Steady," Martin said. "This is no time to panic. Has anyone got him?"

"CQ, CQ, calling CQ, this is 32ZOZ4321—"

"You've drifted again!" Martin screamed.

"Terribly sorry," said 32ZOZ4321. "Over and out."

"Mobile Four reporting. He's turned onto the Via Babuino."

"How'd he get there?" Martin asked after consulting his map. "Has he got wings or something?"

"Correction. I meant the Via Barberini."

"Acknowledged. But how did he get *there*?"

"Mobile One reporting. Target was offered ride by small, fat, bald man driving a blue Alfa-Romeo Model XXV-1 convertible with triple-chromed exhausts and a Morrison-Chalmers supercharger. Target and small, fat, bald man gave the appearance of being friends, or at least acquaintances. They proceeded by various streets to the Piazza di Spagna, where Target disembarked."

"They move fast sometimes," Martin muttered to himself, marking the new location on his map. He said into the microphone, "What did the small, fat, bald man do after that?"

"He drove off in the general direction of the Via Veneto."

"And does anyone have the Target?"

"This is Mobile Two. I've got him. He is presently standing in front, or slightly to the left, actually, of American Express."

"What's he doing?"

"He's looking at a poster in the window. The poster advertises a guided tour of Greece; specifically, Athens, Piraeus, Hydra, Corfu, Lesbos, and Crete."

"Greece!" Martin groaned. "He can't do this to me; I'm not set up for it. We'll have to—"

"Mobile Four reporting. Target is moving again. He has walked several yards and is now sitting on the Spanish Steps."

"You're sure of that?" Martin snapped.

"Absolutely. He is sitting on the seventh step from the bottom and looking in an obtrusive manner at two blonde girls who are seated on the fifth and fourth steps respectively."

"He's trickier than he looks," Martin said.

"Nobody goes to the Spanish Steps any more. I wonder if he's trying—"

"Mobile Three reporting! Target is on the move! He is crossing the Piazza di Spagna. . . . I've lost him. No, I've got him again, he's on the Via Margutta, he's about halfway down the block —he's stopped and turned into a building."

"What building?" Martin screamed.

"The Hunt Club," said Mobile Three. "Shall I follow him in?"

Caroline had been monitoring the search on a monitor. Now she took the microphone out of Martin's hands and said, "Stay wherever you are, all mobiles. I'll pick him up at the Hunt Club."

"Is that wise?" Martin asked her.

"Maybe not," Caroline said, "but it should be interesting."

"Look, baby," Martin said, "the guy is armed and dangerous."

"And attractive," Caroline added. "I want to see for myself what Polletti is like."

"Mr. Fortinbras wouldn't approve," Martin said.

"Mr. Fortinbras isn't killing anybody," Caroline said. "I am."

That was unanswerable. Martin shrugged his shoulders as Caroline walked out. Then he grinned toughly and sagged back wearily in his swivel chair. Prima donnas and incompetents, that's what he had to deal with; people who couldn't organize their way out of a paper bag. He had to do everything. And what thanks did he get for it? None! All he got was the small satisfaction of a job well done.

"All mobile units," Martin broadcast. "Follow Plan Easy-Baker, repeat, Plan Easy-Baker. Over and out."

He walked away from the transmitter still grinning toughly, a dead cigarette hanging limply from one corner of his mouth.

The Roy Bell Dancers had left earlier, and the great ballroom was deserted. The transmitter hummed softly to itself, then crackled. Several seconds passed; then a voice could be heard over the receiver.

"This is 32ZOZ4321 calling CQ. Bob's the handle. Is anyone there?"

There was silence in the great ballroom; eternally, inevitably, no one was there.

11

The Roman Hunt Club was a gracefully proportioned building of neo-barcarole construction. Polletti entered, went past the public rooms, and took the elevator to the third floor. Here he disembarked and walked to a door marked MEMBERS' ANNEX #1 (MEN ONLY). This was one of the few places in Rome where a man could relax, smoke, talk, read newspapers, discuss hunting, and even go to sleep, without his wife's charging in unexpectedly. Furthermore, a man could always *say* he had been there, no matter where he had been. There were no telephones in the room, and the members considered loyalty the greatest of virtues.

Female Hunters had complained about this masculine clannishness and exclusiveness, so the club had given them their very own room on the first floor, marked MEMBERS' ANNEX #2

(WOMEN ONLY). It hadn't satisfied them, really; but, as Voltaire once remarked, what did satisfy a woman, *really?*

Polletti dropped into an armchair and acknowledged the greetings of six or seven friends. They all wanted to know how his Hunt was proceeding, and Polletti told them quite honestly that he hadn't the faintest idea.

"That's bad," said Vittorio di Lucca, a grizzled Milanese with eight kills to his credit.

"Perhaps," Polletti said. "But I'm still alive," he pointed out.

"So you are," said Carlo Savizzi, a plump young man with whom Marcello had gone to school. "But you can hardly take any credit for that, can you?"

"I don't suppose I can," Marcello said. "But there's really nothing much I can do."

"There is a great deal you can do," stated a heavyset old man with grizzled black hair and a face like badly tanned leather.

Polletti and the others waited. The old man was Giulio Pombello, the only Tens Winner that Rome could currently boast. One had to show respect to a Tens Winner even if he talked nonsense, as old Pombello usually did.

"You must organize a defense," Pombello said, waving his right hand defensively. "There are many sound defenses, just as there are many sound Hunting tactics. Selection is of course essential; for example, a Victim must not choose a Hunting tactic, and a Hunter would be ill-advised to think in terms of defense. Do you consider this correct, or have I erred in my grasp of the situation?"

Everyone murmured that the Maestro's words (Pombello liked to be called the Maestro) were apt, skilled, graceful, and definitely to the point. Everyone also wished that Pombello would be struck dumb upon the spot, or receive a telephone call urgently requesting his presence in Corsica.

"So we have reduced the problem to its essentials," the Maestro said. "You are a Victim, Marcello; therefore you need a defense. Nothing could be simpler. It only remains for us to decide which of the many fine defenses available you should select."

"I'm not very defense-minded," Polletti said. "Or offense-minded, either," he added as an after-thought.

The Maestro ignored his words, as he had ignored everybody's words since his tenth kill. "Your best chance," he said, "would be to utilize the Hartman Concentric Field Depth Sequence."

The others nodded slowly. The old man *did* know quite a little about Hunting, when you came right down to it.

"I don't think I know that one," Polletti said.

"It is quite easily grasped," the Maestro said. "First one selects a village of fair size, or perhaps a town. You must be reasonably sure that neither your Hunter, nor his relatives, live in that particular town, since that factor renders the defense ineffective. But a neutral town is not too difficult to find; in fact, the odds are overwhelmingly in your favor."

"It's quite true," Vittorio said. "I was reading just last week—"

"So," the Maestro continued, "having found the town, you go and live there for a week or a month or as long as your Hunter needs to find where you are. Then, when he comes after you, you kill him. It's as simple as that."

Everybody nodded in agreement. Polletti asked, "What happens if the Hunter finds you first, in disguise, perhaps, or—"

"Ah, I see that I left out the key part of the Hartman Concentric Field Depth Sequence," the Maestro said, smiling at his own absentmindedness. "The Hunter *cannot* find you first, no matter how ingenious his disguise. He *cannot* sneak up on you. As soon as he enters the town, he is at your mercy."

"Why?" Polletti asked.

"Because," the Maestro said, "you have previously paid every man, woman, and child in the town to act as your spotters, and you have furthermore promised a bonus to whomever spots the Hunter first. Simple, eh? That's all there is to it."

The Maestro sat back, beaming. The others murmured approvingly.

"You pay every man, woman, and child?" Polletti said. "But that requires a considerable sum of money. Even if it's only a village of a thousand or so inhabitants—"

The Maestro waved his hands impatiently. "I suppose that a few million lire would be needed, paid in advance. But what is that against one's life?"

"Nothing at all," Polletti answered promptly. "But I don't have a few million lire."

"That's unfortunate," the Maestro said. "Hartman's Sequence is, in my personal opinion, the best all-around defense."

"Maybe if I could get some credit—"

"But one need not despair," the Maestro said. "I seem to remember hearing some excellent things about Carr's Static Defense, though I myself have never used it."

"I was reading about it only last week," Vittorio said. "In the Carr Static Defense, one seals oneself into an all-steel room, along with an oxygen regenerator, a water reconstitutor, a generous supply of food, and some good reading material. Abercrombie and Fitch sells a complete outfit, with three-inch-steel hyper-reinforced walls that are unconditionally guaranteed against any explosion up to one megaton."

"Would they sell me one on credit?" Polletti asked.

"They might," Carlo said. "But I'd better warn you that Fortnum & Mason's now sells a multi-wave vibrator unconditionally guaranteed to shake apart anything and anyone inside such a box." He sighed and rubbed his forehead. "That's what happened to my unfortunate cousin, Luigi, on his very first defense."

Everyone murmured his regrets.

"For my part," the Maestro said, "I have never liked the static defenses. They are too static; they lack flexibility. A nephew of mine, however, once used a rather ingenious Defense of Openness."

"I've never heard of that one," Polletti said.

"It's an Oriental form," the Maestro said. "The Japanese call it 'Invulnerability Through Apparent Vulnerability.' The Chinese refer to it as 'The Centimeter Which Contains Ten Thousand Meters.' I believe there is also an Indian name for it, though I cannot remember it at the moment."

Everyone waited. Finally the Maestro said, "Still, names do not matter. The essence of the defense, as my nephew explained it to me, is openness. *Openness!*"

Everyone nodded and leaned forward.

"For his defense, my nephew rented a few square miles of desert land in the Abruzzi, for next to nothing. He put up a tent in the middle of his land. From it, he could see for miles in every direction. He also borrowed a radar set from one of his friends, and bought a brace of antiaircraft guns from a second-hand weapons dealer. He didn't even pay cash for the guns; he merely traded his car for them. I think he also picked up some searchlights from somewhere or other, and he installed the whole thing in two days. What do you think of that, eh, Marcello?"

"It sounds ingenious," Polletti said thoughtfully. "It sounds good."

"I thought so myself," the Maestro said. "But unfortunately, as it turned out, my nephew's Hunter merely bought a surplus tunnel digger from Aramco, tunneled under the boy's tent and blew him to bits."

"Sad, very sad," Vittorio said.

"It was a blow to our entire family," the Maestro said. "But the basic idea is still sound. You see, Marcello, if you took the same concept but modified it somewhat, renting, let us say, a flat granite plain instead of a sand and limestone desert, and if you also installed seismographic equipment, the defense might work very well. It would have certain flaws still, of course; old antiaircraft guns are really not very effective against modern rocketcraft. And there is always the possibility that the Hunter would think to buy a mortar or a tank, in which case the very openness of the defense would be a disadvantage."

"Yes," Polletti said. "And also, I don't think I could make the necessary arrangements in time."

"What about an ambush?" Vittorio said. "I know several superb ambushes. The best of them require time and money, of course—"

"I have no money," Polletti said, rising to his feet, "and I probably have no time, either. But I want to thank you all for your suggestions; especially you, Maestro."

"It is nothing, nothing at all," the Maestro said. "But what are you going to do?"

"Nothing, nothing at all," Marcello said. "One must, after all, remain true to one's basic self."

"Marcello, you are mad!" cried Vittorio.

"Not at all," Polletti said, pausing at the door. "I am merely passive. A very pleasant afternoon to you, gentlemen."

Polletti bowed slightly and left. The others were silent for a moment, staring at each other with expressions of mingled consternation and boredom.

"He is inflicted with a fatal fascination for death," the Maestro proclaimed at last. "This, in my experience, is a typically Roman state of mind against which one must fight with one's entire being. The symptoms of this disease— for it must be so called—are quite apparent to the trained eye; they are, namely. . . ."

The others listened with glazed and vacuous expressions. Vittorio wished fervently that the Grand Old Man would be hit by a car, preferably a Cadillac, and hospitalized for a year or two. Carlo had fallen asleep with his eyes wide open; even in this state he continued to murmur "Hmm," at every break in the Maestro's oration, and to take an occasional puff on a cigarette. He had never revealed to any living soul how he had learned to do this.

12

Caroline lifted her left arm. On her wrist she wore a Dick Tracy watch radio—a family heirloom handed down through generations of Merediths. People were always telling her that she should get a newer, smaller, better watch radio, with additional features and conveniences. Caroline agreed with them in theory, but she refused to part with the antique. It *worked*, she pointed out; and anyhow, she had a strong sentimental streak.

"Martin," she whispered into the watch, "what does *Belleza di Adam* mean?"

"Hang on, I'll find out," Martin said, his voice barely distinguishable over the watch's wretched little speaker.

Martin was back almost at once. "Chet says it means 'The Adam Beauty Parlor,' the same like we got in New York. He says it's the usual sort of deal; Polletti gets his wrists shaved there every couple of days, and then he has lunch or a drink or something in the snack bar."

"Chet sure knows a lot," Caroline said.

"He does," Martin agreed. "As a matter of fact, some people think he knows too much. But why do you want to know about the 'Adam'?"

"Because that's where Polletti is now," Caroline said. "I reached the Hunt Club just as he was leaving, and I followed him to the 'Adam.' But women aren't allowed in a man's beauty parlor, are they?"

"Not in the wrist-shaving section. But the snack bar is open to the public."

"Fine," Caroline said. "I'll go to the snack bar and take a look at him."

"Do you really think you should?" Martin asked. "I mean, maybe it isn't strictly necessary. We've got a couple ideas for getting this joker into the Colosseum tomorrow."

"I know all about your ideas," Caroline said, "and frankly, I don't think much of them. I'll bring Polletti in myself. Besides, I want to get a close look at him. I want to meet him if possible."

"Why?" Martin asked.

"Because it's much nicer that way," Caroline said. "What do you think I am, some sort of pathological murderer? I like to *know* who I'm killing. That's the civilized way of doing things."

"OK, baby, it's your show. But just watch out he doesn't get you first. You're playing with fire, you know."

"I know. But there isn't anything that's as much fun to play with."

Caroline turned off her Dick Tracy watch radio and entered the *Belleza di Adam*. She walked past the wrist-shaving section to the snack bar in the rear. She saw Polletti at once. He had just finished his lunch and was lounging back in his chair with a cup of coffee and a comic book.

Caroline sat down at an adjoining table and ordered a dish of seaweed stew à la Milanese. She took out a cigarette, searched her purse for a light, and turned to Polletti with an embarrassed little smile.

"I seem to be out of matches," she said apologetically.

"The waiter will bring you some," Polletti said, not looking up. He was giggling over his comic book, turning the pages rapidly to find out what happened next, yet reluctant to leave what was behind.

Caroline frowned. She looked adorable when she frowned, as indeed she looked when she did anything. But her beauty was wasted on a man who wouldn't look up from his comic book. She sighed magnificently, and then noticed that each table was equipped with a telephone and a clearly visible number. Smiling piquantly (a thing she did extremely well) she dialed Polletti's number.

His telephone rang repeatedly, but Polletti seemed oblivious to it. Then, at last, he turned directly to Caroline and said, "I told you that the waiter would bring matches."

"Well, it really wasn't *matches* I was calling about," Caroline said, blushing prettily. "The fact is, I'm an American, and I wanted to talk to an Italian male."

Polletti made a gesture with his hands indicating that Rome happened at the moment to be filled with Italian males. Then he turned back to his comic book.

"My name is Caroline Meredith," Caroline said brightly.

"So?" said Polletti, not looking up.

Caroline was unused to this sort of treatment; but she bit her lip charmingly and plunged on.

"Are you free this evening?" she asked.

"I expect to be dead this evening," Polletti replied. He plucked a card from his pocket and handed it to her, still not looking up from his comic book.

The card said: *Be careful! I am a Victim!* It was a standard cautionary note printed in six languages.

"Goodness gracious!" said Caroline in a delectable voice. "A Victim, and you're simply staying out in the open like anyone else! That's a *very* brave thing to do."

"There's nothing else I can do," Polletti replied. "I haven't enough money to organize a defense."

"Couldn't you sell your furniture?" Caroline suggested.

"It's being taken away," Polletti said. "I am unable to pay the installments." He turned a page of his comic book and began to grin.

"Well, goodness," Caroline said, "there simply *must* be something—"

She broke off abruptly at the sound of a sudden commotion. A rat-faced little man had run into the snack bar, crossed it, come to the far wall and turned, his whiskers quivering. Bare moments later a second man entered. He was extremely tall and thin, and his narrow seamed face was tanned the color of a Peruvian saddle.

He wore a very large white hat, a black string necktie, a buckskin vest, Levis, and cowhide boots. He also wore two Colt revolvers slung low on his hips in cut-away holsters.

"Well, Blackie," the thin man said, in a deceptively mild voice, "I reckon we meet again."

"Reckon so," the rat-faced man replied. His whiskers had stopped quivering, but fear was still manifest upon his unpleasant features.

"I also reckon," the thin man said, "that we'll settle this little matter now once and for all."

Caroline, Polletti, and the rest of the diners immediately took refuge beneath the tables.

"There ain't nothing to settle, Duke," the rat-faced man quavered. "There really and truly ain't."

"Is that a fact?" the thin-faced Duke replied, still with deceptive mildness which at this point was deceiving no one. "Wellsir, Blackie, maybe you and me got kind of different values. Me, I'm just old-fashioned enough to resent having my best grazing land cut through by a railroad and my best girl married off to a smooth-talking whiskered little mutt of a Boston banker, and my money taken in a crooked faro game. That's the way I feel about it, Blackie, and I plan to do me something about it."

"Now wait!" Blackie cried desperately. "I can explain everything!"

"Save it," Duke said. "Come on, you high-stepping, fancy-talking, yellow-bellied tinhorn—slap leather!"

"Duke, please, I haven't even got a gun!"

"Then I reckon I'll be the only one to slap leather," Duke said relentlessly. His right hand started to move toward his holster. At that instant the bartender recovered his wits and shouted, "No, no, you must not do that, sir!"

Duke turned to him and said with deceptive mildness, "Sonny, I'd advise you to keep your long nose out of other people's business; otherwise some irate citizen is liable to shoot it off."

"I do not mean to interfere in your affairs, sir," the bartender said. "I merely wished to advise you that murder is illegal in these premises."

"Now look, bub," said the tall stranger, "I'm a fully accredited Hunter and that quivering little rat of a polecat over yonder is my fully accredited Victim. It took a little finagling to pull it off, but I've got the papers all legal-like, so kindly keep out of the line of fire."

"Sir, please!" the bartender cried. "I was not questioning your status. Anyone could see at a glance that you are a man with a perfect right to kill. But unfortunately, these premises have been declared out of bounds for *all* killings, legal or otherwise."

"Well I'll be hornswoggled," said Duke. "First you can't kill in church, then they won't let you kill in a restaurant, then they put barber shops out of bounds, and now *snack bars*. It's getting to the point where a man might as well stay home and die of old age."

"I think perhaps it is not that bad yet," the bartender said soothingly.

"Maybe not, son, but it's getting there. I don't reckon you'd have any objection if I blasted that little polecat in the back alley?"

"We would consider it an honor, sir," the bartender said.

"OK," Duke said grimly. "Blackie, you got

time for one final message to your Maker before.
. . . Hey! Where'd Blackie go?"

"He left while you were talking to the bartender," Polletti said.

Duke snapped his fingers in disgust. "He's a
slippery one, that Blackie, but I'll catch up with
him yet."

He turned and rushed out the door. Everyone
in the snack bar resumed his seat. Polletti resumed
reading his comic book. Caroline resumed looking at Polletti. The bartender resumed making
double Martinis.

Polletti's telephone rang. He waved a hand at
Caroline, vaguely indicating that she should answer it. Pleased and proud at having attained even
this degree of intimacy with her enigmatic
Victim, Caroline lifted the receiver.

"Hello? Just one moment, please." She turned
to Polletti. "It's for Marcello Polletti. Is that
you?"

Polletti turned the last page of his comic book
and asked, "Is it a man or a woman?"

"Woman."

"Then tell her I've just left."

Caroline said into the receiver, "I'm sorry, he's
just left. Yes, that's right, he isn't here. What
do you mean, I'm lying? Why on earth would
I *lie* about something like that? What? What's
my name? My name happens to be none of your
business. What's *your* name? What did you say?

The same to you, sister, in spades! Goodby! What? Yes, *really*, he has *really* just left."

She hung up indignantly and turned to Polletti. His chair was empty.

"Where did he go?" she asked the bartender.

"He just left," the bartender said.

13

Polletti was driving a Buick-Olivetti XXV which he had borrowed from the generous nephew of one of his friend's sister's boyfriends. He hated the car because it was painted fuchsia, a color which Polletti always associated with typhoid fever. Still, it was the only car he could get at the time.

Two miles outside of Rome he pulled into a service station. With a lordly gesture he told the attendant to fill the tank, and then he opened the door and stepped outside.

He heard a wild screech of brakes, turned, and saw a mocha-colored Lotus bearing down upon him. Polletti stood his ground, frozen, not knowing which way to jump even if he had been capable of jumping.

The Lotus swept around him in a perfect Immelman turn and came to a stop. Caroline got out, her musky perfume cutting through the stench of burning rubber.

"Hi," she said.

There were many possible ripostes to a statement like that, but Polletti availed himself of none of them. "Why," he said bluntly, "are you following me? What is it you want?"

Caroline moved closer to him, her perfume like Parthian mead to Polletti's heightened senses. Noticing this, Polletti immediately got back into his car.

"May I have just two minutes of your time?" she asked.

"No."

"One minute?"

"I'm late, I have no time," Polletti said, paying the station attendant and starting his car.

"Listen. . . ."

"Call me next week," Polletti said.

"That'll be too late," Caroline said. "Look, I'm in Rome to make a survey on the sexual behavior of the Italian male. My firm is interested in any unusual aspects—"

"Then you wouldn't want me," Polletti said.

"—but of course we're even more interested in any *usual* aspects," Caroline said quickly.

Polletti frowned.

"Within a definite framework of highly individual particularity, of course," Caroline added. "That's why I'm interested in you. It would be a television interview at the Colosseum. I'd ask you questions—"

"Just me?" Polletti asked.

Caroline nodded.

"I thought you said it was a survey."

"I said it was an *individual* survey," Caroline explained. "An inquiry in depth, a profile approach instead of a surface analysis."

Polletti blinked once or twice. "I don't understand why you want me, in particular, for this interview."

Caroline smiled and turned slightly away. Her voice had a hint of shyness. "It's because I'm drawn to you," she said. "There's something about you—a certain elusive weakness, a tantalizing fragility. . . ."

Polletti nodded understandingly and smiled. Caroline reached for the door handle. Polletti slammed his car into gear and raced off.

14

Polletti drove north on the old coastal road to Civitavecchia, past an endless row of cypresses on his right and a rocky beach to his left. Polletti's mood could be ascertained by the fact that he had the accelerator of his Buick-Olivetti XXV jammed to the floorboard, and he was not planning to let up for any obstacle, animate or inanimate. The fact that the weary old car was incapable of a speed greater than 31 miles an hour made Polletti's gesture poignant, but no less genuine for that.

He came at last to a stretch of beach enclosed by a wire fence. There was a gate, and above it was a sign: THE SUNSETTERS. An attendant came forward and swung wide the portals with a show of deference so great as to be derisive. Polletti nodded curtly and drove in.

He slammed to a stop in front of a little pre-fabricated hut. Past it was a grandstand, partially filled with middle-aged bodies belonging to people of various sexes. Beyond the grandstand was the sea, and just above the water's edge was the fiery red rim of the sun. Polletti checked his watch. It was 6:43 P.M. He entered the hut.

Within was his associate, Gino, seated at a table checking a column of figures.

"How many this time?" Polletti asked.

"Fourteen thousand two hundred and thirty-three paying customers," Gino said. "Also five cops, twenty-three boy scouts, and six of Vittorio's nieces, all on free passes."

"We'll have to tell Vittorio to stop that," Marcello said. "I'm not in this business for my health." He sat down on a camp stool. "Only fourteen thousand? That barely pays the rental on the grandstand."

"It's not like the old days," Gino agreed. "I remember when—"

"Forget it," Polletti said. "Did you check them all for weapons?"

"Of course," Gino said. "I wouldn't want you picked off in the middle of your work."

"I wouldn't either," Polletti said, staring gloomily into space.

There was a short, uncomfortable silence. Then Gino said, "It's 6:47, Marcello."

"Indeed?" Polletti replied cuttingly.

"You must go on soon. You have less than five minutes. How do you feel?"

Polletti could find no words to express his state of mind, so instead he made a bestial face.

"I know, I know," Gino said soothingly. "That's how you usually feel, especially just before you go on. But we can take care of those unhappy, unwanted feelings, eh? Swallow this."

He handed Polletti a glass of water and a tiny red pill shaped like a paramecium. Polletti knew from long experience that it was Limnium, one of the new drugs designed to isolate and energize the so-called 'expansiveness' factor in the human psyche.

"I don't want it," Polletti said, but he swallowed it. Then, resignedly, he swallowed a tiger-shaped purple-and-white-striped pill of Gneia-IIa, the newly modified evoker of charisma developed by I. J. Farben. Then came a little golden sphere of Dharmaoid, the propinquity-perception-reduction agent developed in the Hyderabad Laboratories; then a carefully timed, tear-shaped ampule of Lacchrimol; and at last a wolf-shaped capsule of Hyperbendex, the latest psychic energy energizer.

"How do you feel now?" Gino asked.

"I'll get by," Polletti said. He pursed his lips and glanced at his watch. Then, as the various ingredients hit, he leaped up from the camp stool and bolted to a makeup table in one corner of the hut. He removed his business suit and struggled into a simple white plastic redemption gown, hung around his neck an imitation Mayan sun plaque made of imitation brass, and pulled a curly blond wig over his dark hair.

"How do I look?" he cried.

"Great, Marcello; you look just great," Gino said. "As a matter of fact, you've never looked as great as you look now."

"Do you really mean that?" Marcello asked.

"I swear it by everything I hold dear," Gino said, just as he always said. He looked at his watch. "Less than one minute! Go out there and give it to them, Marcello!"

"I think I shall be sensational tonight," Marcello said, and walked grandly out the door. Gino watched him go, and felt a little throb in his throat. He knew that he was witnessing a real trouper; and he also knew that he was about to have an attack of indigestion.

Polletti marched out grandiloquently to face his audience. His gaze was calm, his step unhurried. Behind and around him the dulcet strains of "O Sole Mio" were diffused upon the still and expectant air.

Nearby was a bit of withered sedge upon which no bird sang. Just past that was a red pulpit to which Polletti repaired. Facing the audience and adjusting the microphone, Polletti declaimed, "Today, at the close of this day like and yet unlike all other days, upon our frail bark of mortality with which we journey across the storm-tossed waters of eternity, we think to ourselves this thought. . . ."

The audience leaned forward expectantly. Polletti saw Caroline smiling at him from the front row. He blinked rapidly once or twice and then recovered.

"These last rays of the dying yet ever-renewing sun," Polletti stated, "come to us from 149½ million kilometers away. What can we derive from this? This distance is supernal and illogical, implacable and yet illusory; for shall not our fiery father return to us?"

"Sure he will!" several thousand voices cried.

Polletti smiled sadly. "And when he returns— will *we* be here to bask in his life-giving splendor?"

"Who indeed can tell whether or not this proposition is true?" the audience responded instantly.

"Indeed, who?" Polletti responded to their response. "Yet we can take comfort in the thought that our dear father has not in fact disappeared at all; that even now he is merely speeding on his urgent journey to Los Angeles."

The sun was sliding beneath the ocean's waves. Most people in the audience were crying, except for an irreducible few who were arguing various sides of the doctrine of solar pseudopropinquity. Even Caroline seemed moved. Polletti himself was in tears as he came to his closing peroration, which he delivered entirely in demotic Greek.

It was completely dark now; and so, to mingled cheers and curses, Polletti left the stage.

A hand seized him in the darkness. It was Caroline, tears running freely down her face.

"Marcello, it was so lovely!" she said.

"I guess it was all right," Polletti said, still weeping, "if you like sunsets."

"Don't you?"

"Not particularly," Polletti said. "I just happen to be in the sunset business."

"But you're crying!" she pointed out.

"A drug-induced response," Polletti told her. He wiped his eyes. "It'll pass soon. One needs to build empathy in this business, and that's hard when one doesn't feel any. But of course, that's business."

"How *is* the sunset business?" Caroline asked.

"It used to be a lot better," Polletti said. "But nowadays. . . ." He stopped and looked at her. "But why are you asking? Is this an interview or just curiosity?"

"Oh, both, I suppose."

"Do you still want that interview with me?" Polletti asked abruptly.

"Of course I do," Caroline said.

"Very well, then," Polletti said, "I'll do it. For a suitable fee, of course."

"Let's say three hundred dollars," Caroline suggested.

Polletti looked blank and began walking to his hut. Caroline followed him, saying, "Five hundred?"

Polletti walked on. With a faint hint of desperation, Caroline bid a thousand dollars.

Polletti stopped. "How long would it take?"

"An hour, two at the most."

"When?"

"Tomorrow morning, at ten o'clock in the Colosseum."

"All right," Polletti said. "I think I'll be free. But perhaps you should put down a deposit to make sure."

Dazed, Caroline opened her purse, took out a crisp $500 bill, and handed it to him. Polletti removed his wig and unzipped a little change purse in the lining. He stuffed the bill in, zipped the zipper shut, and said, "Thanks. I'll see you later."

Coolly he walked on into the hut.

15

Polletti changed into his street clothes and then sat for ten minutes contemplating his right index finger. He had never before realized that it was fully two centimeters longer than his right ring finger. The discovery of this asymmetry, which at another time might have given him a certain wry amusement, now served only to anger him. And his anger in turn served only to depress him, and to produce in his mind images of digital guillotines, ragged-edged hatchets, serpentine yataghans, bloodstained razor blades. . . .

He shook his head violently, pulled himself together and swallowed a stiff dose of Infradex, a drug designed to alleviate drug reactions. Within seconds he was his old, normally depressed self. This cheered him considerably, and he left the hut in a mood teetering on the edge of equanimity.

Outside, in the near darkness, something or

someone touched his sleeve. Polletti's lightning-quick reflexes took over and he whirled into Defensive Maneuver Three, Part 1. Simultaneously, his right hand streaked out like a striking puff adder, snatching for his holstered gun. Unfortunately, he had the bad luck to trip over a cypress root. His hand missed the gun's butt by a mere 1.6 centimeters, and he succeeded only in ripping his jacket as he fell heavily to the ground.

So this is it, thought Polletti. One moment's inattention, and the long expected death came at last—unexpectedly! In that agonized moment, sprawled helpless upon the uncaring ground, Polletti realized that no preparation for one's own death is possible. Death has had too much experience in catching men off guard, in piercing their attitudes and reducing their poses.

All that remained was to die with dignity. Therefore Polletti wiped a fleck of spittle from his lips, choked back an unworthy belch, and smiled with ironic acceptance.

"Goodness," said Caroline, "I didn't mean to startle you. Are you hurt?"

"Nothing is damaged except my self-esteem," Polletti said, getting to his feet and dusting off his clothing. "You shouldn't jump at a Victim like that; you could get killed."

"I suppose I could have," Caroline replied, "if you had gotten your gun out without falling down. You're sort of clumsy, aren't you?"

"Only when I lose my balance," Polletti said with dignity. "Would you mind telling me why you're hanging around here?"

"That's a little hard to explain," Caroline said.

"I see," Polletti said, smiling cynically.

"No, it's not what you think."

"Of course not," Polletti said, smiling even more cynically.

"I simply want to talk with you."

Polletti nodded ironically and smiled most cynically; then, since he detested extremes of attitude, he shrugged ever so slightly and said in a matter-of-fact voice, "All right, I don't care. Let's talk."

They walked together across the low littoral at the sea-down's edge between windward and lee, along the long silver-gray crescent of beach. It was twilight; behind them the eastern sky was blue-black, like a great purplish bruise on the soft white underbelly of the heavens. To westward, the fading colors of the vanished sun's afterglow were drawn irresistibly into the steely waves of the Tyrrhenian Sea. A faint glittering of stars was already visible against the encroaching darkness to the south.

"Gee, those are pretty stars," Caroline said, with unaccustomed shyness. "Especially that little funny one on the left."

"That is U. Cephei," Polletti said. "It's a binary, actually, and its principal star is spectral type B, which corresponds to a surface temperature of some 15,000 degrees."

"I never knew that," Caroline said, sitting down on the close-grained sand.

"U. Cephei's small companion," Polletti went on, "has a surface temperature of only six thousand degrees, give or take a few degrees." He sat down beside her.

"That's sad, in a way," Caroline said.

"Yes, I suppose it is, in a way," Polletti said. He felt strangely lightheaded. Perhaps this was because the star he had so confidently identified as U. Cephei was in fact Beta Persei, also known as Algol, the Demon Star, whose autumnal effect upon certain temperaments is too well known to be discussed here.

"Stars are nice," Caroline said. It was the sort of statement which Polletti would usually have considered banal, but which now he found endearing.

"Yes, I suppose they are nice," he replied. "I mean, it's nice to have them there every night."

"Yes," Caroline said. "It's very nice."

"It really is nice," Polletti agreed. Then he got a grip on himself and said, "Look, we didn't come out here to discuss stars. What do you really want to talk about?"

Caroline didn't answer at first. She was looking pensively out to sea. A long tress of blonde hair had fallen across her cheek, softening and framing the exquisite line of her face. Dreamily she picked up a handful of sand and let it run through her long, slender fingers; and Polletti, cynic though he was, felt a sudden irrational pang of sentiment run through the very depths of his being. Absurdly enough, he found himself remembering a little thatched house in the hills above Perugia, and a plump, gray-haired, smiling woman standing in the vine-shrouded doorway with an earthenware pitcher in her hand. He had seen that motherly figure only once, on a postcard which Vittorio had sent him. It had made no impression on him at the time; but now. . . .

Caroline turned to face him, and her great violet eyes reflected the last rosy glint of afterglow. Polletti trembled, though the sea-level temperature was 78° Fahrenheit and a sultry breeze was blowing from the southwest at five miles an hour.

"I want to know about you," Caroline said simply.

Polletti managed to laugh. "Me? I am a very usual sort of man, and I have lived a very typical life."

"I want to hear about it," Caroline said.

"There's really nothing to tell," Polletti said; but he found himself talking about his childhood, and his first boyish experiments in murder and sex; his confirmation, and the days of his young manhood; his infatuation with serene and optimistic Lidia—an infatuation which marriage had transformed into a crescendo of boredom; his meeting and subsequent life with Olga, whose hectic wildness he learned too late was due to a congenital instability rather than to a passionate independence of character.

Caroline realized at once that, for Polletti, experience had brought only the bitter residue of pleasure which is the true essence of disenchantment. Certain delights which in his youth had seemed unique and unobtainable had turned out, upon acquisition, to be infinitely and drearily repeatable. Through this morose insight he had wrapped himself in that civilized gray cloak of ennui which some say is but the reverse side of the piebald garment of hope. It was sad, she thought; but surely not irrevocable.

"And that's it, that's everything," Polletti said, a little defensively. He realized that he had been babbling like a moonstruck adolescent. But he sternly reminded himself that it was not important, that he didn't care what Caroline thought of him.

Caroline said nothing at all. She was turned toward him, her face hidden and mysterious in the clinging darkness, a faint nimbus of starlight outlining her hair. She leaned almost imperceptibly closer to him, and her sweetly curved body and imagined face seemed archetypical rather than individual. She was perhaps a great beauty;

but darkness rendered her lovelier still through Polletti's imagination.

He stirred restlessly. He reminded himself that the disillusioned, through the very specialization of their attitudes, are frequently and peculiarly prone to the myth of romance. He lit a cigarette and said, "Let's get away from here. Perhaps we could go somewhere for a drink."

His matter-of-fact words were meant to break the spell. They failed, for Algol was still burning in the southern sky. Caroline said, in a voice barely louder than the low murmur of the surf, "Marcello, I think I love you."

"Don't be ridiculous," Polletti said, trying to subdue an anticipation of ecstasy by a show of irritation.

"I do love you," she said.

"Forget it," Polletti said. "This beach scene is all very pleasant, but let's not get carried away."

"Then you love me, too?"

"It doesn't matter," Polletti told her. "At the moment I could say almost anything, and believe it—but only for the moment. Caroline, love is a wonderful game which begins in fun and ends in marriage."

"Is that so bad?"

"In my experience, yes, very bad indeed," Polletti said. "Marriage kills love. I will never marry you, Caroline. I will never marry anyone again. I consider the entire connubial institution a farce, a travesty on human relations, a wicked trick with mirrors, an absurd self-imposed trap—"

"Why must you talk so much?" Caroline asked him.

"I'm naturally loquacious," Polletti said. It suddenly seemed very natural to be holding Caroline in his arms. "I love you very much," he told her. "I adore you, Caroline, against all my better instincts."

He kissed her, tenderly at first, then with increasing passion. He found that he did indeed love her, and this surprised him, delighted him, and saddened him. For love, as he knew it, was an aberration, a form of temporary insanity, a short-lived state of autosuggestion.

Love was a state which a wise man would prudently avoid. But Polletti had never considered himself wise, and prudence was the least of his virtues. He was unashamedly self-indulgent —which was in itself a possible form of wisdom. Or so he hoped.

16

It was deepest night in the Colosseum; a black and unforgivable night, clinging like seaweed to the ancient stones, its awesome integrity broken only by several banks of arc lights which made the place brighter than day.

Down below, on the flat blood-drinking sands, half a dozen cameramen stood by their cameras. The Roy Bell Dancers, on a special platform to left of center, were resting after their latest rehearsal, and talking about ways to prevent the ends of one's hair from splitting. Not far from them, in a motor coach filled with controls and instruments, Martin sat and made a final check of camera angles. He had left the Borgia Ballroom and transferred to this, his new command post. He had a thin black cigarette clenched between his teeth. Occasionally he reached up and rubbed his watering eyes.

Chet sat behind him in front of a little table. The fact that he was playing solitaire showed the terrific nervous tension he was undergoing.

Cole was seated just behind Chet. The fact that he was dozing uneasily in his chair showed the terrific nervous tension *he* was undergoing. He woke up abruptly, rubbed his watering eyes, and said, "Where is she? Why doesn't she report?"

"Take it easy, kid," Martin said, not looking around. The fact that he was compulsively rechecking all his camera angles for perhaps the hundredth time showed that even he was not immune to the anxieties of other, lesser men.

"But she should have reported by now!" Cole said. "Do you suppose. . . ."

"I don't suppose anything," Martin said, and directed Camera 3 to pull back one and two-thirds inches.

"Black ten on red jack," Cole remarked to Chet.

"Suppose you keep your nose out of my personal business," Chet said, mildly, yet with a deep-seated hint of violence.

"Easy, kids," Martin said softly. A natural-born leader of men, he knew by instinct the proper moment for a reassuring word instead of an angry command. Nervelessly he now directed Camera 1 to tilt down one and three-quarters degrees.

"But she should have reported by now!" Cole

said. "She hasn't reported since she arrived at the Sunsetters Beach. That was six or seven hours ago! She hasn't answered our calls. Anything could have happened—anything, I tell you! Do you suppose. . . ."

"Get a grip on yourself," Martin said coldly.

"Sorry," Cole said, putting both trembling hands to his white face and rubbing his aching eyes. "It's the tension, the waiting. . . . I'll be all right. I'll be fine once the action starts."

"Sure you will, kid," Martin said. "The waiting gets to us all." He barked into his microphone, "Hold that tilt, Camera 1, and come back exactly one-half inch; and damn you, *steer small!*"

"Red two on black three," Cole remarked to Chet.

Chet didn't answer. He had decided to kill Cole immediately after he had gotten Martin fired. He had also decided to kill Mr. Fortinbras and Caroline, and his brother-in-law in Kansas City, Missouri, who invariably greeted him with a cheerful, "How's it going with the image maker?" And also. . . .

The door of the motor coach opened and Caroline walked in. "Hi, troops," she said cheerfully.

"Hi, kid," Martin said casually. "How'd it go?"

"Smooth as Acrilan," Caroline replied. "I caught his act, and then I talked to him and he agreed to the interview tomorrow."

"Have much trouble?" Chet asked mildly.

"Nope. He came across without much persuading, very businesslike about the whole thing. Five hundred down, five hundred in the morning before the interview starts."

"Fine, great, good," Martin said. "But what did you do *after* that? I mean it's been about five hours since you were supposed to report, and we were naturally worried about you."

"Well," Caroline said, "I started to leave, but then I decided that maybe I should size him up a little more. So I went back and asked him out for a drink, and after that we went to this lovely little beach and talked and looked at the stars."

"That's nice." Martin smiled, a nervous tic developing at the corner of his left eye. "And how did you size him up, hmmmm?"

"He's a wonderful man," Caroline said dreamily. "But you see, he's been trying to get his marriage annulled for twelve years, and during that time he's been living with this madwoman named Olga, and now that he's finally got his annulment he doesn't want to marry Olga."

"That's very interesting," Martin said.

"As a matter of fact, he doesn't want to marry anyone," Caroline said. "He doesn't even want to marry me."

Chet sat up so abruptly that he upset his cards. "Hey, what is this?" he asked.

"I guess maybe you could call it like love," Caroline said.

"Whaddaya mean, *love*?" Chet asked. "Your contract expressly forbids you to fall in love during the duration of your tenth kill, and it furthermore explicitly forbids you to fall in love with your Victim."

"Love," Caroline said coolly, "existed a long time before contracts."

"Contracts," Martin said viciously, "are a lot more enforceable than love. Now look, baby, you aren't going to chicken out on us, are you?"

"I don't suppose so," Caroline said. "He said he loved me, too. . . . But if he won't marry me, I guess he's better off dead."

"That's the spirit," Martin said. "Just remember that, okay, kid?"

"I'm not likely to forget it," Caroline said coldly. "But do you suppose. . . ."

"I don't suppose anything," Martin said. "Look, let's all go get ourselves a little shuteye, be nice and fresh for the morning's kill. Right? Right."

All agreed. Martin gave the orders, and the arc lights slowly faded. The cameramen and the dancers left. Last of all, Martin, Chet, Cole, and Caroline left, got into Martin's rented Roadrunner XXV, and drove off to their hotel.

Black and impenetrable night lay over the

Colosseum, its gloom pierced only by occasional cloud-smothered glances from a horned and gibbous moon. Silence oozed from the ancient rocks, and the sensation of impending death rose like an unseen miasma from the bloodsoaked sands.

Then Polletti stepped from beneath an archway. His face was stern and angry. Behind him came Gino.

"Well?" Polletti asked.

"It's clear," Gino said. "She's your Hunter. There can be no doubt."

"Of course not. I was sure of it when she followed me out to the beach. This is merely confirmation. A big kill with plenty of publicity—the American style!"

"I hear they're doing it that way up in Milan now," Gino said. "And of course the German Hunters, particularly in the Ruhr—"

"Do you know what she told me tonight?" Polletti said. "She told me she loved me. And all the time she was planning to kill me."

"The treachery of women is proverbial," Gino said. "What did you tell her?"

"I told her of course that I loved her," Polletti said.

"Do you, by any chance?"

Polletti thought for a long time. Then he said, "It's odd, but she's actually very lovable. She's a nicely raised girl, quite shy in many ways."

"She's killed nine men," Gino reminded him.

"You can't really hold that against her," Marcello said. "That's simply a manifestation of the times."

"Perhaps you're right," Gino said. "But what will you do, Marcello?"

"I shall perform the counter-kill, exactly as I had planned," Polletti said. "The only real question is whether Vittorio has been able to arrange any publicity in time."

"You didn't give him much notice," Gino said.

"That couldn't be helped," Polletti said. "He should be able to line up one or two sponsors, anyhow."

"He'll probably arrange something," Gino agreed. "But Marcello, what if she suspects that you've caught on? She has a big organization behind her, money, power. . . . Maybe you should just kill her at the first opportunity and take no chances."

Polletti drew a revolver from his jacket pocket, checked the load, then put it away. "Don't worry," he said to Gino. "She's coming to my hut at nine in the morning for a rehearsal. Does that sound as if she suspects me of suspecting her?"

"I don't know," Gino said. "I only know that the treachery of women is proverbial."

"So you told me," Polletti said. "But then, so is the treachery of men. It'll go off just as I've planned. I only wish she were less lovable."

"It is the lovability of women," Gino stated, "that exposes us to their treachery."

"I suppose so," Polletti said. "Anyhow, I'm going back to the hut. I need some sleep. You make sure that Vittorio makes sure of the arrangements."

"I'll do that," Gino said. "Good night, Marcello —and good luck."

"Good night," Marcello said.

They left. Marcello got into his car and drove back to the beach, and Gino walked to the nearest all-night café.

And now at last, the Colosseum was deserted. The moon had waned and darkness was over all. A faint mist had sprung up, and faint cloudy figures seemed to move over the kill-crazy sands like the ghosts of long-dead gladiators. A breeze sighed across the empty seats like the voice of a long-dead emperor murmuring, "Do him in!" And then, out of the ambiguous gloom of the east, the first lightening of the morning sky could be discerned.

An uncertain new day had begun.

17

Within his prefabricated hut, Marcello was sleeping deeply and well. He did not hear the faint squeak of hinges as his door was cautiously pushed open. Nor did he see the long, oddly shaped muzzle pushed in through the partially opened door.

The muzzle centered on his head. There was a faint hiss, and a barely visible rush of gas escaped from the muzzle. Immediately, Polletti's sleep became even deeper.

A few seconds passed, and then Caroline stepped into the hut. She touched Polletti lightly on the shoulder, then shook him. Polletti didn't stir. Caroline walked back to the door and waved. Then she came back into the room and sat down on the bed beside him.

The hut began to shake and quiver. It leaned sharply to one side, and Caroline had to hold

Polletti to keep him from falling to the floor. After a few moments the hut stopped moving.

Polletti was still asleep. Caroline went to the door and opened it. She could see the streets of Rome gliding past. It would have been an eerie sensation if Caroline had not known that the hut, with herself and Polletti in it, was tied onto the bed of a truck, which Martin was presently driving toward the Colosseum. It was 8:46 exactly. Caroline searched the hut, took care of a few minor matters, and then sat down beside Polletti.

About half an hour later, Polletti stirred, rubbed his eyes, and sat up. "What time is it?" he asked Caroline.

"Nine twenty-two," Caroline said.

"I'm afraid I overslept," Marcello said.

"It doesn't matter."

"But do we still have time for the rehearsal?" Polletti asked.

"I'm sure we'll do all right without it," Caroline told him. Her face was hard, and she spoke quietly, without emphasis. She turned away from him now and began to make up her face with the help of a tiny compact.

Polletti yawned and reached for his telephone. Then he noticed that the wire was cut. Caroline was watching him in her compact mirror. Polletti stretched, apparently at ease, and reached for his

142

jacket on a nearby chair. He took out cigarettes and matches, and patted the breast pocket. His revolver was no longer there.

Lighting up, he gave Caroline an affectionate little smile. Receiving no response, he leaned back in bed, drew deeply on his cigarette, then turned over and found his little electronic monkey on the floor. He played with it for a while, then climbed quickly out of bed and changed into slacks and a sport shirt. He lay down on the bed again and picked up the monkey.

Caroline still had not turned to look at him. She was still watching him in the mirror of her compact.

Polletti stretched out again on the bed. "Do you know what I was just thinking?" he asked her. "I was just thinking, why don't you and I go away somewhere—just the two of us. We could have a wonderful life together, Caroline. We could even get married, if you thought it absolutely necessary."

Caroline closed her compact and turned to face him. She held the compact in her hand, one finger poised over the back hinge. It was doubtless a gun, Polletti decided. It was hard nowadays to find anything that wasn't a gun.

"You're not interested in my offer?" Polletti asked.

"I'm not amused by your lies," Caroline told him.

Polletti nodded, playing with his electronic monkey. "You may be right," he said. "I've done too much lying and cheating in my time. Not through fondness for falsehood, I can assure you; just through—circumstances. But I do want to be honest with you, Caroline. I *can* tell the truth. Perhaps I could even prove my sincerity."

Caroline shook her head. "It's too late."

"Not at all," Polletti said. "I have friends who will vouch for my character. For example—" he held up the electronic monkey—"have you met Tommaso?"

"That's just the kind of character witness you'd have," Caroline said.

"Tommaso is a very truthful little beast," Polletti said. He put the animal on the floor and turned it to face her. The electronic monkey hopped over to her and tried to climb up her leg.

"I'm not interested in him," Caroline said.

"But you aren't being fair. Look how affectionate he is. I think he likes you. Tommaso is very choosy about his friends."

Caroline smiled with evident effort, then lifted the monkey and set him on her lap.

"Stroke him," Polletti suggested. "And you might also pat him on the nose. He likes that very much."

Caroline turned the animal over. Then, gingerly, she patted his nose.

The electronic animal abruptly stopped moving. Simultaneously, a panel in his chest swung open, revealing a heavy revolver concealed inside.

"Did you know about this?" Caroline asked.

"Of course," Polletti said. "Just as I know about you—that you are my Hunter."

Caroline stared at him, the smile gone from her face.

"That revolver is proof of my sincerity," Polletti said. "It is proof that I want to live with you . . . that I do not want to kill you."

Caroline bit her lip. Her face set, and her hand tightened over the revolver within the electronic monkey.

Just at that moment the walls of the hut began to tremble violently, and then to rise slowly into the air. Caroline did not even bother to look up at this unusual sight. Her intent gaze never left Polletti's face. Polletti, for his part, watched with evident delight as the walls lifted, foot by foot, revealing rows of ruins in the middle distance.

"It's wonderful, Caroline," he said. "It's absolutely marvelous."

Now the upper part of the hut was lifted away entirely. Gazing skyward, Polletti could see the walls being borne away in a south-southwesterly direction on the end of a single-core Nylorex cable by a helicopter painted red, white and beige —the colors of the UUU Teleplex Ampwork.

And around him, tier upon crumbling tier, rose the serried bleachers of the Colosseum.

Cameras swung in, ridden to earth by men in baseball caps. Microphones dangled over Marcello's head like a cluster of surrealistic bananas. The Roy Bell Dancers received a standby signal. Red lights blinked like the malignant eyes of Cyclops, and Martin's voice could be heard barking orders in a jargon so technical that only Chet was able to understand it and transmit it to the proper recipients.

Polletti watched this spectacle within a spectacle with something not far from incredulity, though not from belief, either. He turned to Caroline and asked lightly, "Shall I say a few words into the microphone?"

Caroline regarded him with eyes like milky obsidian. "There's only one thing you have to do: die!" She had a revolver trained on him now. It was Polletti's own weapon, taken from his jacket pocket inside the hut.

The orchestra (the Zagreb Philharmonic had been hired especially for this occasion) now burst into a lilting, ominous *paso doble*. The Roy Bell Dancers stopped discussing hair sprays and exploded into a mellifluous, perilous *danse du ventre*. The cameras rolled in and out on their long skeletal booms like crazed giant praying mantises.

More signals were flashed. From his waiting

position beneath a crumbling arch, a uniformed attendant wheeled out a little table containing a teapot and a cup of tea, all real except for the prepackaged vapor which rose from the cup. On his way out, the attendant almost collided with a slim, dark, elegant young woman, exquisitely though somewhat theatrically dressed, with the large, black, shiny eyes of a jacklighted wolf.

"A typical homicidal schizophrenic paranoid, and with kittenish overtones yet," the attendant muttered to himself, completely unaware that the woman was Olga, and that his diagnosis of her contained more truth than poetry, and more verity than wit.

"Tea!" remarked Polletti, when the attendant reached him. "Must I drink it?"

"*She* drinks it," the attendant whispered. "You just stand there and die good and don't be a wise guy." He turned on his heel and left; he had the real professional spirit, and he hated levity.

"Uncle Ming's Terrific Tea!" cried an announcer from a different part of the Colosseum. "Yes, ladies and gentlemen, Uncle Ming's Terrific Tea is the only tea which adores you for yourself alone, the only tea which would gladly marry you and raise little tea bags if only Uncle Ming would allow it."

Polletti laughed with delight. He had never heard this particular advertisement, which last year had won the triple goldburst decoration from the Advertising Council, Inc., for propriety, taste, humor, originality, and many other virtues.

"What's so funny, Marcello?" Caroline asked, hissing the words like a deadly spotted adder from central Borneo.

"It's all funny," Polletti said. "I tell you that I love you, that I want to marry you; and you turn me down by killing me. Isn't there something humorous about that?"

"No," Caroline said. "Not if you really mean it."

"Of course I mean it," Polletti said. "But don't let that stand in your way."

"—and so, out of the depths of its tortured, hopeless infatuation, Uncle Ming's Terrific Tea cries out to you: 'Drink me, Mr. Consumer, drink me, drink me, drink me!" the announcer concluded. His message was followed by a moment of stunned canned audience disbelief, and then by a few tentative canned handclaps, and at last by a stunning canned audience ovation.

"Double handful to splashout!" Martin called.

"Ten seconds to go," Chet translated. "Nine, eight, seven—"

Caroline stood like a statue except for the tremors of tension that ran down her right arm and imparted to the muzzle of the tightly gripped revolver a barely perceptible vibration.

"—six, five, four—"

Polletti stood his ground easily, the smile on

his face conveying his sense of amusement at the alien yet thoroughly human drama in which, unaccountably, he found himself a prominent actor. (The smile also conveyed a sense of uncharacteristic patience, an innate feeling for propriety, and a pathetic little string of veal between his third and fourth canines.)

"—three, two, one, fire!"

Caroline shuddered throughout her entire being at the tremendous irreversibility of the instant. She raised her revolver slowly, falteringly, like a maniacal sleepwalker awakened into a nightmare. She pointed the gun at Polletti's head, centering an inch above his eyebrows. Instinctively she took up the slack in the trigger pull.

"Splashout! Splashout!" Martin screamed.

"Fire! Fire!" Chet screamed in translation.

"Execute soonerest!" Martin roared.

"Do it now!" Chet roared in translation.

But nothing moved in the murderous tableau. The tension of that moment was almost beyond description. Indeed, susceptible young Cole keeled over in a faint; Chet was stricken with a temporary (but nonetheless painful) paralysis of the right biceps, triceps, and lateral extensors; and even Martin, hardened professional though he was, felt a twinge deep in his throat which he knew to be the unmistakable onset of heartburn.

Directors and cameramen waited; the Roy Bell

Dancers and the Zagreb Philharmonic waited; the vast worldwide audience waited, except for an irreducible few who had gone into the kitchen for a beer. Polletti waited; and Caroline, torn by indecision and wracked by ambiguity, found herself waiting for *herself* to act.

How long this might have continued is hard to estimate; but suddenly, an imponderable element entered the unpredictable equation. Olga ran out from beneath the arch, burst through the anxious little crew of technicians, vaulted to the floor of the hut and snatched the revolver out of Caroline's hand.

"So, Marcello," Olga said, "I find you again with another woman!"

There was no response to this lunatic statement, which carried with it, as the statements of the insane all too frequently do, the definite impress of a subterranean truth.

"Olga!" Polletti cried, vainly hoping to explain the inexplicable.

"After twelve years of waiting," Olga cried, "you do *this* to me!" And she leveled the revolver at a spot approximately one inch above Polletti's eyebrows.

"Please, Olga don't shoot!" Polletti pleaded. "It will be worse for you if you do. We can talk about this rationally—"

"I have already had a *rational* talk today—with Lidia!" Olga declared. "Your former wife admitted that the annulment had come through—not today, not yesterday, but *three days ago!*"

"I know, I know," Polletti said. "But I can explain everything. . . ."

"Then explain this!" Olga screamed, and pulled the trigger.

The gun barked with deadly authority. Olga gasped in amazement, put a faltering hand to the region of her heart, looked with disbelief at the blood on her fingers, and then slumped over, dead as a pterodactyl in a glass case.

"This *will* be difficult to explain," Polletti conceded.

Caroline sat down on the bed and clutched her head. Cole came out of his faint and thought to himself with pride, "Gee, I actually fainted." Chet went to black and switched over to a stand-by film: *The Big Telecast of 1999.*

Starring Le Mar deVille, Roger Roger, and Lassie.

Martin walked over to the hut, took in everything at a glance, and asked, "What's going on around here?"

A policeman came up, failed to take in everything at a glance, and asked, "Who is the Hunter, please?"

"I am," Caroline said, holding out her identification card but not looking up.

"And who is the Victim?"

"I am," Polletti said, also holding out his card.

"Then this dead woman was not in the Hunt?"

"No," Polletti said.

"In that case, why did you kill her?"

"Me? I haven't killed anybody," Polletti said. He bent down and picked up the revolver. "Look," he said to the policeman, and showed him the small opening just below the hammer.

"I see nothing relevant," the policeman said.

"That hole is the revolver's real muzzle," Polletti said. "The gun fires backward, do you understand? It's my own invention; I built this myself."

Caroline stood up quickly and glared at Polletti. "Why, you animal!" she cried. "You planned for me to steal that gun out of your jacket! You gave it to me so that I would kill myself!"

"Only if you happened to try to kill me," Polletti pointed out.

"Words, words!" Caroline screamed at him. "How can I believe anything you say to me?"

"We'll discuss it later," Polletti assured her. "My love, there is a simple explanation for all of this—"

"Which," the policeman interrupted rudely, "you will first have to try on *me* before insulting the young lady with your spurious harlequinade." He smiled gallantly at Caroline, who frowned at him.

"First I shall inform headquarters," the policeman said, unclipping his portable radio from his pistol belt, "and then I shall expect to hear some answers."

Neither of these expectations came to pass, however; for the policeman found himself abruptly and desperately engaged in trying to maintain some faint semblance of order.

First there were the tourists, several thousand of whom had broken through the restraining cordon outside of the Colosseum, and all of whom were determined to find out what was going on and to snap a picture of it. Next, clawing through the tourists, came the lawyers, several dozen of whom had arrived miraculously on the scene, and who were variously threatening suit against Polletti, Caroline, the UUU Teleplex Ampwork, Martin, Chet, the Roy Bell Dancers, Cole, the police of Rome, and other—unspecified —parties. Finally there were six officials of the Hunt International. They demanded that Caroline and Polletti be taken into immediate custody, pending charges of unjustifiable nonmanslaughter.

"All right, all right," said the overtaxed policeman, "first things first. I shall arrest the alleged Hunter and her alleged Victim. Where are they?"

"They were standing here just a moment ago," Cole said. "Do you know, I actually fainted earlier?"

"But where are they now?" the policeman asked. "Why wasn't anyone watching them? Quick, guard all the exits! They can't have gotten far!"

"Why couldn't they have gotten far?" Cole asked.

"Don't provoke me!" the policeman roared. "We shall soon find out if they have gotten far!"

And soon—but not soon enough—he found out.

18

Guided by Caroline's skilled hands, the small helicopter, previously overlooked in a corner of the great stadium near Trajan's arch, soared high above the city of Rome. The yellow-gray oval of the Colosseum dwindled out of sight. The dense and circuitous streets of the Eternal City gave way to suburbs, and then to villages, and then to open countryside.

"You're marvelous!" Polletti declared. "You planned it this way all along, didn't you?"

"Of course," Caroline said. "It seemed a reasonable precaution to take, just in case you were telling the truth."

"My darling, I can't tell you how much I admire you," Polletti said. "You have snatched us from death and lawsuits, into the magnificent open air, into the wilderness, far from electric razors and refrigerators. . . ."

Polletti glanced over the side and noticed that they were over a bleak, whitened desert, toward the lunar face of which the helicopter was beginning to descend.

"Tell me, my treasure," Polletti said, "do you have anything else planned for us?"

Caroline nodded gaily and brought the helicopter to an adroit landing. "Mainly *this*," she said, seizing Polletti and kissing him with the enthusiasm and *élan* which she brought to most things.

"Mmmmm," Polletti said, then raised his head abruptly. "That's strange," he said.

"What's strange?" Caroline asked.

"I must be having an hallucination. I thought I heard a church bell."

Caroline looked away with that droll hint of coquetry which characterized even her simplest movements.

"I did hear it!" Polletti said. "There it goes again!"

"Let's take a look," Caroline said.

Hand in hand they left the helicopter, walked around a small rocky ledge, and found themselves standing less than 20 yards from a little church neatly built into the overhanging granite of the hillside. In the doorway of the church was the black omnipresent figure of a priest. He smiled and beckoned to them.

"Isn't it nice?" Caroline said, tugging at Polletti's hand and leading him forward.

"Charming, fascinating, unusual," Polletti said, his voice marked by a slight but decided loss of its previous gusto. "Yes, decidedly engaging," he said in a somewhat stronger tone, "but not entirely credible."

"I know, I know," Caroline said. She led Polletti into the church and up to the altar. She knelt before the priest; after a moment, Polletti also knelt. Organ music issued forth from nowhere. The priest beamed, and began the ceremony.

"Will you, Caroline, take this man, Marcello, as your wedded husband?"

"I will!" Caroline said, with fervor.

"And will you, Marcello, take this woman, Caroline, as your wedded wife?"

"I will not," Polletti said, with conviction.

The priest lowered his Bible. Polletti saw that the man had marked his place with a .45 caliber Colt automatic.

"Will you, Marcello, take this woman, Caroline, as your wedded wife?" the priest repeated.

"Oh, I suppose so," Polletti said. "I had merely wished to wait a few days so my parents could attend."

"We'll get married all over again for your parents," Caroline assured him.

"*Ego conjugo vos in matrimonio . . . ,*" the priest began.

Caroline quickly gave Polletti a ring, thus enabling them to exchange rings in the classic old ceremony which Polletti had always found so moving. Outside, the desert wind moaned and complained; inside, Polletti smiled and said nothing.

———————